OVER THE EDGE!

Nancy's body dropped like a lead weight. She bounced against the side of the cliff and began to slide. Her arms instinctively reached out and clutched with all their strength at a thick protruding root. Her feet dangled below her.

Nancy looked down. At the bottom of the long dropoff, a pile of boulders awaited her. She swallowed hard, willing herself not to think about what would happen if she fell.

But her hands were starting to slip on the dirt-encrusted root. "Frank! Joe!" she called out. "Help!"

"Anchor me!" Joe ordered his brother. As Joe lay flat on his stomach, leaning over the edge, Frank grabbed his ankles. He dug his own heels into the ground for support.

Joe reached down, the tips of his fingers a foot away from Nancy's. With a sudden jerk, Nancy slipped a couple of inches down the root.

"I can't hold on!" she cried.

Nancy Drew & Hardy Boys SuperMysteries

Available from ARCHWAY Paperbacks

A NANCY DREW & HARDY BOYS Super Mystery™

BURIED IN TIME

Carolyn Keene

AN ARCHWAY PAPERBACK
Published by POCKET BOOKS
New York   London   Toronto   Sydney   Tokyo   Singapore

AN ARCHWAY PAPERBACK *Original*

An Archway paperback published by
POCKET BOOKS, a division of Simon & Schuster Inc.
1230 Avenue of the Americas, New York, NY 10020

ISBN: 0-671-67463-3

First Archway Paperback printing August 1990

10 9 8 7 6 5 4 3 2 1

Printed in the U.S.A.

IL 7+

BURIED IN TIME

Chapter

One

Ugh! Who turned off the air-conditioning?" George Fayne asked.

A wall of hot air hit Nancy Drew as she followed her friend George through the airport exit. In front of her a brightly painted sign said Welcome to Oklahoma! "Whew! Some welcome," she said, brushing a lock of red-blond hair off her forehead.

The harsh rays of the late-morning sun beat against the two girls, and they dropped their bulky duffel bags on the sidewalk. At the curb a line of people were climbing into a bus with the name of a rental-car agency printed on its side.

"Maybe we should go with them," George said, nodding toward the air-conditioned bus. "I think your dad's friend forgot about us."

Nancy checked the area out for anyone who fit her father's description of Tod Langford. He was a thin, tanned, forty-five-year-old professor with salt-and-pepper hair, a gray beard, and wire-rimmed glasses. He'd been a college friend of Carson Drew's, but they'd gotten out of touch—until Langford made a frantic phone call to Carson the day before. Something about mysterious thefts at an archaeological dig site. Langford needed someone to investigate—right then.

Carson had apparently sent his old friend a Christmas card the winter before, mentioning his daughter's work as a detective. In any case, Langford wanted Nancy for the job because she and George were the right age to pose as volunteer diggers.

"Let's give him a chance," Nancy said. "Dad said the dig site is a three-hour drive from here. Maybe he got stuck in traffic."

"Uh-huh," George said. "Either that or his car melted. I can't believe how hot it is here." Her eyes quickly refocused on something behind Nancy. "Speaking of hot—"

Nancy turned around. Jogging toward them was a tanned, athletic-looking young man dressed in khaki shorts and shirt. His wavy

2

dark hair fell in strands across his handsome face.

"That can't be him," Nancy said.

"Excuse me!" the guy said, stopping beside them. "Let's see—reddish hair, blue eyes, tall, slim. Are you Nancy Drew?"

Nancy and George exchanged a brief look. "Yes," Nancy replied as he stopped in front of them.

"And I'm George Fayne," George quickly added.

"George?" the guy said with a puzzled smile, extending his hand.

George took it and smiled warmly. "Short for Georgia."

"But you're not Professor Langford?" Nancy questioned.

"No." The guy's smile broadened, revealing one small dimple on the left cheek. "No, I'm Jim Haber, his graduate assistant. He sent me to pick you up. Sorry to keep you waiting. I was sitting at the wrong terminal for half an hour." He gave an embarrassed shrug. "Let me help you with your bags. My car's in the lot."

He lifted both duffel bags, and the three of them walked toward the short-term parking lot. "You're an archaeologist, Jim?" George asked.

Jim laughed. "I know, I know, I can spot a tiny piece of clay pottery in the middle of a desert, but put me in an airport and I get lost—"

"No, I didn't mean it that way!" George replied. "I was just, you know, interested."

Nancy sighed to herself. She could tell by George's tone of voice that she was interested, all right—interested in Jim Haber. George was usually a no-nonsense, level-headed person, but every once in a while a cute guy could make her act a little—well, different. And then Nancy could see the resemblance between George and her boy-crazy cousin, Bess Marvin. Nancy would never admit this to George, though.

Jim led them to a silver pickup truck and threw the duffel bags in the back. "Where's yours?" he asked George.

"Huh?" was all George could say.

"Your luggage," Jim said. "Both of these say Nancy Drew on them."

"Oh!" George replied. "I borrowed one from Nancy. Mine ripped on a camping trip."

Jim smiled. "An outdoorsperson—that's great. Half of our volunteers have never been outside a suburb." He hopped into the driver's seat, and Nancy and George squeezed in next to him.

"If you need anything—suntan lotion, light clothing, bathing suits—we can go into Oklahoma City now," he continued, starting up the engine. "The summer can be pretty brutal, and once we get to Quartz Mountain, we're in the middle of nowhere. How long did you sign up for?"

"Till Nancy finds—" George began.

"It's open-ended," Nancy interrupted, silencing George with a look. Langford had asked that Nancy and George's mission be kept secret. Everyone at the dig was supposed to think that they were volunteers. "Since it's our first time, we want to see how we like it."

"Right," George said sheepishly.

"That's good," Jim replied. "Keep your options open. Some volunteers end up making a career out of it. Others bag out in August when it starts getting hot."

"Starts?" George said. She held her short, dark curls off her neck with one hand, fanning herself with the other.

Jim chuckled. "It's not as bad as you think. There's great waterskiing on Lake Altus, hiking trails on Quartz Mountain—"

At the mention of athletic activities, George's brown eyes lit up. All her fears about the bad weather seemed to magically melt away.

As Jim drove onto the highway, the three of them chatted comfortably. Before long the suburban sprawl outside Oklahoma City gave way to flat, sparse countryside. They passed one-street towns, ranches that stretched to the horizon, and prairies dotted with clumps of sagebrush.

"This was all American Indian territory," Jim said at one point, gesturing out the window. "Then, about a hundred years ago, the United States government declared the first Oklahoma Land Run. White settlers rushed in, and towns sprang up overnight. Tribes that had been here for centuries were forced to scatter, some of them leaving no traces—"

"But others did," Nancy chimed in, "and those are the ones you're digging to learn about."

"Not exactly," Jim replied. "The tribe we're trying to learn about disappeared centuries before that—and I mean *disappeared*. We know they were incredibly powerful in their time, but all of a sudden—poof! They were gone. Or so we thought. When we discovered this site about six weeks ago, none of us could believe it. The artifacts all seem to belong to this long-lost tribe. We think our site was their main burial ground. You guys are lucky—you could become part of history."

Unless someone steals the history from under our noses, Nancy thought.

Quartz Mountain looked like an enormous pile of granite boulders that had been swept into the middle of the prairie. Smaller hills, speckled with brownish green grass, lay on either side of it. Between the hills, Nancy caught a glimpse of a silvery lake. In the dry southwestern heat, the water shimmered like a mirage.

The pickup bounced along an unpaved road, sending up a cloud of dust. As Jim pulled to a halt, he said, "Last stop. Welcome to our grand headquarters."

Just beyond the settling dust, Nancy could see a weather-beaten gray tent. In front of it, three young, sunburned volunteers took swigs from their canteens. Their bare shoulders were peeling, though it was hard to see their skin through the layers of reddish brown dirt that covered them.

Nancy and George climbed out of the pickup and followed Jim into the tent. "I have to warn you," he said, pulling the tent flap aside. "This is going to be hot and it isn't pretty."

He was right. Nancy almost passed out from the heat-saturated air inside the tent. Broken pieces of pottery covered every flat surface— two rickety card tables, a long desktop held up by metal file cabinets, the floor, the coffee table, the sofa. But Nancy noticed there was a curious order to the chaos—each fragment was carefully labeled with a small index card.

Through the middle of the fragments, a narrow pathway had been left that led to a large folding table. Behind it, a middle-aged man sat on a canvas chair, examining a fragment with a magnifying glass. He appeared to be unfazed by the heat.

"Dr. Langford!" Jim called out cheerfully. "The new recruits are here!"

Langford looked up. His thinning hair was a dusty color, and his gray-green eyes seemed like beacons nestled in his dark, sun-bronzed skin. As he stood up, a smile crinkled across his face. "At ease, lieutenant," he said to Haber with a chuckle. Turning to Nancy and George, he extended his hand. "You'll have to excuse my eager young assistant. I think he picks up the military jargon from the guys over at the air force base."

"That's okay, we're used to him already," Nancy answered, smiling.

After Jim introduced them all, Langford led them outside. "Let's not waste any time. I'd like to show you the site. Jim, would you take their bags over to the resort?"

"Sure thing," Jim said. He fished out a set of keys from his pocket and gave it to Nancy. "You're in room two-oh-eight at the Quartz Mountain Resort. It's only a few minutes' walk from here."

"Thanks," Nancy said.

Jim threw the duffel bags in the pickup and drove off while Nancy and George followed Dr. Langford around to the back of the tent.

"I'll let you get settled in a few moments—I promise," he said, leading them up a gently

8

sloping hill. "First I want to tell you what I know about the vandalism—"

"Dr. Langford!" came a shout from above them.

All three looked up to see a young, curly-haired volunteer calling down to them from the top of a hill. "Come quickly!" he urged.

"What is it, Max?" Langford called out, already breaking into a sprint.

"One of the trenches," Max said, his eyes wide with fear. "It just—collapsed!"

Chapter

Two

Wᴵᵀᴴᴼᵁᵀ ᴬᴺˢᵂᴱᴿᴵᴺᴳ, Langford sprinted up the hill. Nancy and George could barely keep up with the professor's bounding steps.

George was the first to the top after Langford. She stopped short and let out a low whistle of amazement.

Nancy ran up beside her and looked down the opposite side of the steep cliff. In the claylike soil below was a vast pattern of long trenches and deep holes. Ladder tops peeked out of the holes, and shovels and pickaxes lay strewn about. Along the sides of the trenches were piles of pot fragments, bones, and a few skulls.

"Are they—human?" George asked.

"Come on!" Nancy urged. Langford and Max were already halfway down, rushing along a winding trail.

Nancy and George followed. As they neared the bottom, Nancy spotted their destination. At the base of the cliff, not visible from above, a long trench was filled with rubble. A ladder stuck out of one side; the other side was caved in. Next to the ladder a dozen or so people were huddled in a circle.

When Langford approached them, the circle opened. In the middle sat a bare-chested digger, clutching his foot.

"Are you all right, José?" Langford asked as Nancy and George ran up behind him.

"Just a sprained ankle," José replied. "I was lucky. When the side started crumbling I was already halfway up the ladder."

Langford studied the trench. "Was anyone else inside?"

José shook his head. "I was the last one out."

Whispering in the crowd made Nancy look up. A stern-looking middle-aged man pushed through, his brow creased. The red shine of his balding scalp was brighter than his loud Hawaiian shirt, and on a leather string around his neck hung a forest of possessions—a magnifying glass, keys, a Swiss army knife, and a gold medallion or two. "What happened here?" he asked, kneeling next to José.

"I'm all right, Dr. Ottman," José replied, beginning to look a little embarrassed by all the attention.

As Ottman and Langford helped him up, Nancy wandered around the edge of the trench. Her footsteps sent up little clouds of reddish dust from the parched soil. Beyond the crowd, the ground was smooth and untouched, interrupted only by small clumps of snakegrass. She walked around to study the cave-in, on the side opposite the ladder.

The collapse had eroded the edge of the trench back six feet or so. Loose rubble, which had avalanched into the trench, was piled on a slant back up to where Nancy knelt. There were sharp, vertical marks in the ground near her. They looked as if someone had been shoveling. Nancy's blue eyes narrowed thoughtfully.

The sound of footsteps made her raise her head. George was approaching her.

"For goodness' sake!" Langford's voice boomed from across the trench. "Get away from there, you two! You want to fall in?"

As he sprinted toward them, Nancy and George took a few steps back. "Sorry," Nancy said to Langford, "but are those marks supposed to be there?"

Dr. Langford lowered his gaze. With a frown, he moved toward the marks. "That's strange—"

"Tod!" Dr. Ottman called, waving Langford over. "Where'd you go? Give me a hand here!"

Langford continued staring at the marks until Ottman called out again. "Be right there!" Langford finally replied. Turning to Nancy, he said, "Don't go too far. I need to talk to you."

George waited until Langford was out of earshot, then asked, "What's going on?"

"Look at this," Nancy replied.

George stared at the spot. "The trench collapsed—I could see that from the other side."

"But these are shovel marks, George."

"Right," George said, not understanding Nancy's point. "I didn't think they used their *hands* to dig these things."

Nancy gestured down the length of the trench. "Look how straight the rest of the edge is—and see where the marks are. But here somebody started shoveling a few feet away from the trench, which weakened one of the sides. *That's* what caused the collapse." She stood up and began walking away.

George went with her. "You think someone sabotaged it?"

Nancy shrugged. "It's possible. We'll have to find out what Dr. Langford thinks."

The crowd was beginning to disperse. A couple of people were helping José over to a pickup truck. Others were starting back to work. Still others were heading toward Nancy and George to check out the collapse.

That was when Nancy noticed them—the two very familiar faces.

"Frank and Joe Hardy?" she said under her breath. What were they doing *here?*

George squinted against the rising sun. Despite the glare, there was no mistaking the two Hardy brothers—the six-foot blond with the rippling muscles was Joe, and the dark-haired guy, who stood six-foot-one, was his brother, Frank. Frank was staring straight at Nancy.

Nancy opened her mouth to call out to them but stopped short. There was a firm, piercing gaze in Frank's eyes that said, "Pretend we don't know each other."

Nancy turned away. She pulled George away a couple of steps, and they walked past Frank and Joe with nothing more than a friendly nod.

"Hey, what—you didn't even say—" George protested.

"Shhh," Nancy said. "They don't want us to know them."

"What? Did you and Frank have a fight or something? Don't tell me you—"

Nancy shook her head. "No, George!" She knew just what George was implying. Nancy and Frank's minds always seemed to be in sync, even when they hadn't seen each other for a while. There was a bond between them. Not that it was serious or anything—Nancy had her boyfriend, Ned Nickerson, and Frank had his girl, Callie Shaw. But George liked to tease Nancy about Frank, which didn't matter to Nancy, since there wasn't a grain of truth to it.

Well, maybe *half* a grain . . .

When they got out of earshot, Nancy said, "They must be incognito—and so must we, remember?"

"Sure, but it seems stupid to just ignore them. Maybe they're here for the same thing! We could work together."

"I didn't say we were going to ignore them. We just have to meet them in a way that doesn't make anyone suspicious."

George nodded. Her eyes wandered over to Frank and Joe's group. A few feet from them a pair of sunglasses lay on the ground. "Don't look now," she said, "but I think we have our opening."

"The old drop-the-handkerchief trick," Nancy said with a laugh. "Leave it to Frank and Joe."

"The what trick?" George asked.

Nancy began walking. "You know, like the old movies. A girl wants to get a guy's attention, but she doesn't want to be obvious. So she drops a handkerchief"—she leaned over to pick up the glasses—"and the guy feels it's his duty to return it. Only this time the handkerchief is a pair of sunglasses. And Frank's the girl in this movie, and we're the guy—"

George rolled her eyes. "I don't like the way this sounds."

"Excuse me!" Nancy called out as she approached the group. "Do these belong to any of you?"

They all turned. Frank raised his eyebrows and replied, "Oh, they're mine! I must have dropped them."

Nancy stopped herself from cringing. Frank wasn't going to win an Oscar for his acting, that was for sure. She smiled pleasantly and held out the glasses.

Frank took them and, nodding to her and George, said, "Thanks!" Then, under his breath, he added, "Dinner at the resort restaurant, six-fifteen."

"Okay," Nancy murmured. Then, in a clear voice, "You're welcome."

"Hey, she's pretty, but couldn't you think of something less obvious than that?" a smiling red-haired guy said behind Frank. "Like just saying 'hello'?" The group broke out laughing.

"You don't know him," Joe said good-naturedly. "He's just naturally clumsy."

They laughed again, and Frank pretended to be embarrassed. One by one the guys introduced themselves to Nancy and George.

"Were any of you working in this trench?" Nancy asked.

"I was," said the red-haired guy, whose name was Saul.

"What do you think caused the cave-in?" Nancy continued.

Saul shrugged. "Who knows? These things happen. Maybe there was a fault in the soil—"

"Maybe revenge from the dead," said another volunteer.

"The dead?" Nancy said, puzzled. "Is this a grave?"

"Yep," Saul said. "We finished clearing out the bones yesterday."

"Oh, nice," George said, barely concealing her distaste. "I'm glad you told me that."

"The thing is," Saul continued, "this tribe buried a lot of their treasures with their dead. All kinds of gold and silver jewelry, pottery, carvings—really sophisticated stuff."

Which might give someone a reason to commit robbery, Nancy thought, but not a reason to sabotage the site. This case seemed to be more serious than a theft. Nancy wanted to talk to Langford quickly before somebody got hurt.

"Well, we better get our assignments, George," Nancy said. "See you guys."

"So long," said Saul.

Frank and Joe, who had been silent the whole time, waved goodbye with the others.

Walking to the other side of the trench, Nancy spotted Langford. He was giving instructions to several of the diggers.

A clatter of hooves made Nancy turn around. Across the plain behind them, a horse was approaching at full gallop. On it was a young Native American woman, her long hair flowing behind her like black satin ribbons. As she got closer, Nancy could see anger burning in her eyes.

Langford barely noticed the young woman as he continued giving instructions to several of the diggers. "Sarah, you and John see about clearing out the rubble. Be careful—I don't want you damaging the artifacts *or* yourselves. Charlie, get the traffic cones from the lean-to and spread them around the cave-in. All of you who were working here at Site Seven should divide yourselves around the other sites, okay? Come on, look alive!"

As the volunteers obeyed him, the young woman brought her horse to a halt right next to him. He appeared to be startled.

The young woman glowered down at Langford. Her chestnut brown horse snorted a couple of times and shook its head.

A chill went up Nancy's spine when she heard the young woman's first words. "Bad things happen when you disturb the sleep of the dead, Dr. Langford!"

Chapter
Three

THE YOUNG WOMAN sat in silence as if waiting for an answer. Langford's eyes shifted nervously.

"Er—Nancy, George," he said, "this is Red Sky Winsea."

"Hi, Red Sky," Nancy said uneasily.

The young woman's expression softened as she took in Nancy and George. "Call me Sky," she said with a trace of a smile. "I don't recognize you. You must be new to the dig."

"Just got here," George replied.

"Well, you'll be seeing a lot of me," Sky said.

Langford cleared his throat. "Sky's grandfa-

19

ther owns this land," he explained. "He leased it to us for the dig."

"And you know who gets the better end of *that* deal," Sky interjected.

Langford exhaled. It was clear he and Sky had had this conversation before. "Your grandfather is being compensated very well for the use of the land. You of all people should know that."

Sky's eyes instantly flashed with anger. "No compensation is enough, Dr. Langford. I've been telling you that since your dig began. The dead are sacred to us. When you start disturbing the remains of our ancestors, you are killing our souls."

"Sky, they're not your ancestors," Langford protested. "This was never Comanche territory. These people were totally unrelated to you."

"It makes no difference. You are desecrating Native American graves, and for what? To find potsherds, to rob the dead of their possessions and their dignity—to steal our past as if it belonged to you!"

"Potsherds?" George whispered to Nancy.

Sky heard her question and answered, "Little pieces of pottery. Toys for the archaeologists. They piece the pots together like puzzles, study the secrets of the craft, write articles, then pat themselves on the backs and give one another more grants to dig even more."

20

Dr. Langford sighed. "Sky, I understand what you're saying, but——"

"No," Sky interrupted with intensity, "as long as you continue to dig, you *don't* understand. And I will do my best to make life difficult for you."

She yanked the reins sharply to the left. Her horse reared briefly, let out another little snort, then carried her back across the plain.

Dr. Langford seemed to be embarrassed as he watched the horse and rider recede in a trail of red dust. "Sorry about that," he said with a shrug. "I do respect her point of view, but I have to be true to the principles of my profession."

Nancy and George both nodded, both unsure of how to react.

"Anyway," Langford went on, "let's get started, shall we?"

Nancy and George followed him to another rectangular trench, wider and deeper than the first. The bottom lay in the shadow of the steep sides, but Nancy could make out a treasure trove of artifacts. A carved wooden pipe was lined up next to a couple of small statuettes of eagles and foxes, grimacing with oversize mouths. Bone jewelry and head ornaments, painted with reds and yellows that had almost faded to shades of brown, lay about in neat piles. In one corner was a gargantuan, grinning mask with a stiff but perfectly preserved animal pelt hanging from it.

"Voilà, the treasure of the Red Clay Vaults —and these are just the things we've found today!" Langford said with pride. "The key to an entire lost culture. I mean, the Spiro influence is undeniable, but there's a clear metamorphosis into a new society—evident, for example, in the almost totemic symbols!"

Nancy and George shot each other looks of confusion. "Dr. Langford," Nancy said, "you just lost me. First of all, who is Spiro?"

Langford chuckled. "Sorry. I forgot I was talking to laypeople. Spiro was the name of one of the major southwestern tribes of antiquity. Master traders, exquisite artists—they had everything going for them. They ruled an empire so vast it may have stretched from the Great Lakes to Central America. Their art and culture probably influenced the Mayas and the Aztecs. And then—" He shrugged his shoulders. "As all cultures eventually do, theirs fell apart. Probably they had gotten too big. Their centralized government couldn't control the foreign elements that were seeping into their outer territories."

George shook her head. "And these are their remains—the Spiro's?"

"Well, not exactly," Langford said. "The evidence tells us that many Spiro were conquered by a warlike tribe from western Oklahoma. They were brought here and forced into slavery, and their captors took all their riches. We don't even know the name of the captors—I call them the Red Clay People." He kicked up a cloud of red dust. "For obvious reasons."

"If the tribe that conquered the Spiro was so powerful," Nancy asked, "how come you don't even know its name?"

Langford shrugged. "It has been one of the major anthropological mysteries of the Southwest. Until we stumbled on these graves, we had hardly a trace of this warrior tribe. Many of my colleagues don't believe the Red Clay People even existed." He smiled triumphantly. "My work on these graves will change all that."

"Some graves," Nancy remarked. "They look like little underground museums."

"You're right. I call them vaults because they contain such an incredible wealth of history. Many ancient peoples buried treasures with the dead, as offerings to their gods. The Spiro did, and I imagine their conquerors adopted the tradition. This must have been the main burial ground for the Red Clay People— maybe the only one in the country!"

"Sounds pretty important," George volunteered.

"Important?" Langford laughed. "It's only one of the major discoveries of the twentieth century. We'll be able to fill in major gaps in the history of the Spiro. And we'll begin to see what their conquerors were like. These last six weeks will mean more to my career than anything in my entire twenty-odd years as an archaeologist!"

"I can't imagine how you ever found this place," Nancy remarked, gazing out across the desolate landscape. "Was it just guesswork, or did you find a stray potsherd or something?"

Langford's eyes shifted. "Oh, you know—poking around, talking to people. It just happened," he said vaguely. Then he shrugged. "Anyway, the important thing here is the vandalism. As you can see, the trenches are wide open and unguarded. It has always seemed a little absurd to hire a guard in the middle of these plains. It's not like there's a gang of criminals lurking around the nearest corner."

Nancy peered down into the red clay vault. "What exactly was taken?"

"From this one? A couple of animal-tooth necklaces," Langford answered. "From Vault Two, a few ceremonial bracelets. Some pottery and tools are gone from Vault Five."

"Does it seem like the thief is familiar with the site?" Nancy asked.

"You mean, was it done by an insider?" Langford asked. "I just don't know. The thief would have to go pretty far away to hide his stuff, let alone sell it. So if anyone left the site, everybody else would notice."

"If it were done by a stranger, you'd probably notice the person right away," George said.

"Unless he sneaked in and out at night," Langford replied. "Except for the really large pieces, we take all our new finds into the tent to be catalogued at the end of each day. So the things must have vanished during the day. Anyway, I haven't finished telling you the whole story. You see those two holes over there?"

He pointed to a couple of partially dug trenches a few yards away.

"You mean those new ones?" Nancy asked.

"They're actually old ones," Langford said. "Vaults Four and Nine. They were filled in last night."

"Filled in?" George exclaimed. "Why would anyone—"

Langford sighed. "My question exactly. At first I thought the thief was doing it to cover his tracks—"

"But he stole from Vaults One, Two, and Five, and he didn't cover them up," Nancy said.

"Good deduction. That's why I brought you here," Langford said. With a weary smile, he glanced at his watch. "I'm supposed to be back at my tent to meet with Dr. Ottman right now. Can we continue this first thing tomorrow morning—say, seven o'clock, before the hordes get here? There are still some important things to discuss."

"Fine," Nancy replied.

"Good." He turned to go, then called over his shoulder, "Feel free to look around all you want."

"Thanks," Nancy said. Grabbing the ladder into Vault One, she began climbing down. "Come on, George."

George watched Langford disappear over the hill, then climbed in after Nancy. "Do you get the feeling he doesn't really believe in us?" she asked.

"Sort of," Nancy said. "But to tell you the truth, I'm not sure I believe in him."

"Why?"

"Something about the way he talks, I guess. And he's got a huge ego. I think he thinks he's much smarter than anyone else."

" 'Good deduction!' " George said, imitating Langford's voice.

"And then the way he reacted, or rather didn't react, to those shovel marks at Vault Seven," Nancy added. The girls were on the dark floor of the gravesite. "There was something he wasn't telling me, I'm sure."

"Well, he couldn't be the thief, right?" George asked. "I mean, he's the one who brought us in."

Despite the shadowy darkness, it wasn't much cooler down in the vault. A musty smell permeated the stagnant air, and the sudden skittering of a lizard made Nancy jump.

"Watch it, Nancy!" George shouted suddenly.

Nancy spun around and gasped. A face, half-human and half-eagle, leered down at her through bulbous yellow eyes.

After a moment Nancy sighed with relief. The thing wasn't alive—it was a mask!

"Don't do that to me, George," Nancy said.

"Sorry," George replied. "For a minute there I honestly thought it was alive."

Nancy smiled and turned away. "Come on, let's check out some of this stuff."

As she knelt beside a pile of potsherds, though, Nancy could still feel the creature glaring at her. No matter where she went, the eagle's eyes seemed to follow. Soon Red Sky Winsea's words began echoing in her head: "Bad things happen when you disturb the sleep of the dead."

Nancy tried to shake off her fear. It was ridiculous to be afraid of spirits, she told herself. Sky wasn't above suspicion herself; the mysterious saying might have been a smoke screen.

Still, though, George was right. The eagle figure did seem to be alive. It looked as if it wanted to chase them away. And Nancy felt like taking the hint.

At six-thirty that evening the sun cast long shafts of light through the windows of the Quartz Mountain Resort restaurant. Nancy and George carried their food trays through the cafeteria section that had been set up especially for Oklahoma University personnel. As they headed toward the patio just outside the kitchen door, the tangy smell of her burrito-and-enchilada combo made Nancy ravenous.

"There they are," George said, nodding toward a picnic table at the edge of the patio.

Rising from the table, Frank and Joe waved them over. Nancy and George sat on the bench opposite them.

"Couldn't resist the two hottest-looking girls on the dig," Joe said with a mischievous smile. "How nice of you to allow us the pleasure of your company."

Frank rolled his eyes. "Ease up, Joe," he muttered.

"I just don't want anyone to think we know them," Joe whispered.

Nancy glanced around. The tables were spaced far apart, and everyone on the patio seemed to be involved in conversation. "I'm sure you have everyone here totally fooled," she said with a reassuring smile.

"What I want to know," Frank said, leaning across the table, "is if you're here for the same reason we're here."

Nancy leaned across the table to face him eye to eye. She felt a small glow of pleasure at the sight of his dark eyes and handsome features. "That depends," she said, matching his tone, "on the reason you're here, doesn't it?"

Now it was George's turn to roll her eyes. "Ugh, competition between detectives. Just what we need."

Frank, Nancy, and Joe all laughed. Checking right and left to make sure they hadn't gotten anyone's attention, Nancy asked Frank, "How did you hear about the thefts?"

She was met by blank stares from both brothers. "Thefts?" Frank repeated.

"Yes, you know, the—" Nancy paused and sat back. "I guess we *are* here for different reasons!"

"Actually, we're based in Altus," Frank said, "But we're thinking of staying at the resort here. We came to check it out. When we got here, we thought we'd check out the dig, too—and the rest is history!"

"Our, uh—group sent us on an assignment," Joe explained. "We're supposed to track down a couple of big truck shipments that disappeared about two months ago. No one else has had any luck finding them."

Nancy knew that the Hardys' "group" was a

secret intelligence agency called the Network, known only to a handful of people in the country. Sensing that George was about to ask about it, Nancy suddenly felt uncomfortable.

Frank saw what was happening and spoke right up. "Two unmarked trucks," he said. "One carrying heavy water and one carrying a load of uranium two-thirty-five."

"The last checkpoint for both shipments was the Jackson Air Force Base," Joe added. "Just outside Altus."

"Heavy water—uranium—" Nancy let the sound of those words sink in. She had read those terms in the science section of the newspaper, and they gave her a chill. "That can mean only one thing, right?"

Frank and Joe were nervous.

"What?" George said, perplexed. "What am I missing here?"

Nancy exhaled. "Those two things," she said, measuring her words carefully, "are used to make nuclear weapons!"

Chapter

Four

O<small>H, GREAT</small>," George said. "I thought we'd be doing a little detective work, a little horseback riding—now we're in the middle of a nuclear war!"

"Whoa, I wouldn't go that far," Joe protested.

"Hey, I've seen enough TV to know what goes on out here," George replied. "Missile silos, underground command centers—"

Frank sighed. "Let's put this into perspective, okay? Yes, it's possible that's what the stuff is being used for, but our sources say that there aren't any known terrorists in the country with the expertise to make a nuclear bomb. It's possible the materials were illegally dumped, or something got fouled up at another checkpoint, or the trucks got lost."

"What if your sources are wrong, though?" Nancy asked. "I mean, about the terrorists."

Frank sighed. "Well, I guess that's why it's so urgent for us to find the stuff and return it."

The table fell into glum silence for a moment. Then Joe broke it. "So—what were you saying about thefts?"

Nancy was happy to change the subject. "Someone's been snatching ancient Indian artifacts from under the noses of the entire archaeological team," she answered. "And someone, maybe the same person, has been sabotaging the trenches."

"Any suspects?" Frank asked.

"A couple," Nancy replied. "There's Red Sky Winsea, the granddaughter of the guy who owns the land—"

"I saw her when she rode in," Joe butted in. His blue eyes had a flirtatious gleam in them. "I'll investigate her personally, if you want."

"Big of you, Joe," Frank said, slightly annoyed. "I know what a sacrifice it would be—going after a mysterious, gorgeous dark-haired girl on horseback."

Before Joe could protest, Nancy said, "Seriously, you guys, it wouldn't be a bad idea if we helped each other out, worked together."

Frank nodded. "Just as long as we keep the Lone Ranger in line."

Nancy looked at Joe and saw that his face was turning beet red. She couldn't help but laugh, and George joined her.

"Hope I'm not barging in on anything," came a male voice from behind Nancy.

They all turned to see Jim Haber approaching with a full dinner tray. "Hi, Jim!" George called out. "Come sit with us." She scooted over, crowding Nancy.

George asked if the Hardys knew Jim. They introduced themselves. Jim settled in. "So, you survived your first day of Oklahoma heat?"

"No problem!" George answered with a big grin. "Great tanning weather."

Joe raised his eyebrows ever so slightly and gave Nancy a brief, triumphant look—a look that said, "See? I'm not the only one."

"Turns out you got here just in time for the excitement, huh?" Jim said, plunging his fork into a taco salad. "The cave-in, the thefts— much more interesting than your typical dig."

"Mm-hm," Nancy said casually, cutting her burrito into small pieces. "I can't imagine who could be doing it. Everyone around here seems so honest and friendly."

"Except for that strange woman on horseback," Frank said with a sidelong glance at his brother.

"Ease up, huh?" Joe said.

"Do you have any ideas about it, Jim?" Nancy asked.

"Not really," Jim replied, staring at his plate intently. "I guess you never know."

"What do you mean?" Nancy pressed.

Jim shrugged. "I don't know. You just— never know." His face was stiff. "So," he said, taking in Frank and Joe and obviously trying to change the subject, "you two are new to the dig? I'm surprised Dr. Langford didn't tell me you were coming."

"Nope, we're just traveling through, thinking of staying at the resort," Frank said. "We checked out the dig earlier today, and now Nancy and George are trying to convince us to stay on."

"Well, new hands are always welcome," Jim said pleasantly.

Small talk continued to flow. Nancy was determined to bring up the crimes again, but it took Jim only a few minutes to finish his meal. Wiping his mouth, he hopped up from the table. "Well, *hasta mañana,* folks," he said. "You guys may get to relax at the end of the day, but I have to catalogue artifacts." He whisked his tray off the table and walked away.

"He inhaled that taco salad," George remarked.

"Yeah," Joe said with a raised eyebrow, "a

person can get pretty hungry dodging questions."

Nancy nodded. "I noticed that, too."

"Hey, you don't suspect Jim, do you?" George asked in disbelief.

"Maybe you should interrogate him while Joe goes after Sky," Frank suggested.

"Very funny," George replied, scowling.

Nancy leaned her elbows on the table. "I think we'd better figure out what to do next." She leveled her gaze at Frank. "What are your plans?"

"We paid for one more night in Altus," Frank answered, standing up with his tray. "Can we meet you here tomorrow morning?"

"Great," Nancy said. "In the meantime, we'll listen for anything about the radioactive stuff."

Joe grinned irrepressibly. "Yeah, let us know if anybody's hands glow in the dark."

With that, the Hardy brothers left the table and headed back into the cafeteria. Nancy noticed the frown on George's face. "What's the matter?" she asked.

"I didn't like that comment," George replied.

"About the radioactivity?"

"No, about interviewing Jim. What does Frank think I am, some lovesick groupie?"

"Don't worry about it, George," Nancy

said. She took a last bite of her food and washed it down with some diet soda.

George crumpled her napkin onto her tray and stood up. "I mean, I do think the guy is nice and all, but that's *my* business."

Nancy heaved a sigh. Maybe this case was going to be even harder than she'd thought.

Promptly at seven the next morning, Nancy and George trudged over the hill to the site. As the sun rose in front of them, Nancy felt as if it were prying her eyes open.

"If I could see, I'd probably think it's very beautiful out here," George said, in a voice groggy from sleep.

Nancy grunted in agreement, still trying to wake up. When they had left the resort minutes before, they were the only ones awake. Yet as Nancy peered down on the dig site, she could see four people.

Three of them were police officers, standing in front of two Jeeps with police department logos on their doors. Next to them, Jim Haber was gesturing toward one of the vaults—or what was left of it.

"Uh-oh, looks like another collapse," George said.

Nancy felt suddenly alert. She began hurrying down the hill. "This is getting out of hand," she called over her shoulder. "We may have to camp out at the site nights."

"Oh, that'll be fun," George replied, following behind. "We can have pajama parties with the evil spirits."

At the bottom of the hill, Nancy could hear Jim saying, "It could have been anytime, officer. Late night, early morning—he's unpredictable."

A burly police officer scribbled something on a pad. From his chiseled features and pitch-black hair, Nancy guessed he was at least part Native American. Looking up at Jim, he said, "I'd have these trenches inspected if I were you."

"Thanks," Jim said flatly. "I'll do that."

A young female police officer walked up to the first officer. "Lieutenant Deerhunter," she said, "we've got the owner coming over now. Sergeant Mendez is at the resort talking to Dr. Ottman."

Deerhunter glanced briefly at the hill and closed his notebook. "Want to join us?" he asked Jim.

"Sure, in a minute," Jim replied softly, his voice hesitating. "You go ahead."

As the officers walked toward their cars, Jim turned to Nancy and George. Despite a deep tan, his face looked ashen.

"Was this the only one?" Nancy asked, pointing at the vault.

Jim was silent. Although he was only a few feet away, he seemed not to hear her.

"Jim?" George said. "Jim, are you all right?"

"I'm fine." Jim's answer came out as a ghostly whisper. "But Dr. Langford is dead."

Chapter

Five

A TUMBLEWEED BOUNCED toward them, brushing lightly against Nancy's leg before it went on. "Dead?" she said, shocked. "What happened?"

Jim exhaled heavily and rubbed his forehead. "I—I don't know. Two of the volunteers found him about an hour ago, half-buried in Vault Thirteen. Looks like it collapsed on him."

"Oh, no," George murmured.

Nancy felt weighted down with horror. She struggled to think clearly, sorting out the questions that flew around in her head. "Why were those volunteers here?" she finally asked.

"They're staying next door to Tod in the hotel," Jim answered. "Tod's alarm radio went off full-blast this morning and it didn't stop. The guys got curious when they knocked on his door and he didn't answer, so they went to find him—" He cast a sad glance toward the vault. "And they found him, all right."

"Why would he have been here?" Nancy asked.

Jim shook his head. "Who knows? He was an insomniac. Sometimes I'd hear him wandering around the resort in the middle of the night. Maybe last night he took a walk out here."

Nancy looked into the trench. Its south wall was now an avalanche of red soil, covering about half the width of the trench floor. At the bottom, the smooth slope of the soil was interrupted by frantic digging marks where Langford's body had been pulled out.

"So that was it, huh?" Nancy said. "He suffocated?"

"Or had a heart attack," Jim replied. "I guess there'll be an autopsy to determine the exact cause." His eyes began to mist over. "But it doesn't matter, does it? He's gone."

"Jim—" George said gently, taking his arm.

Jim forced an awkward laugh. "I'm all right. It's just that we had gotten pretty close. I mean, he was a tough guy to get along with, but he was a brilliant archaeologist. And we worked well together." He pulled his arm free of George's hand. "Well, I'd better get to the tent to join the police before they send a posse for me."

"We'll come with you," George said.

As they climbed the hill, George stayed close to Jim. At the top, they could see a throng of people outside the headquarters tent. Word must have spread at the resort. The two police Jeeps were now parked near the tent, at the edge of the crowd, next to a tangle of low, thorny bushes.

A distant clopping of hooves made Nancy turn. She saw a pinto horse approach, carrying an old, upright, white-haired man with a ponytail. Nancy watched the man dismount and pull the horse's reins over its head. He wore a fringed white cotton shirt, embroidered with colorful designs in a zigzag pattern.

The hubbub of voices grew louder as Nancy, George, and Jim moved closer to the crowd. Near the tent door, Lieutenant Deerhunter was questioning one of the volunteers, who looked shaken. Deerhunter nodded patiently as the skinny, dark-haired guy stammered nervous answers. "We—we just, you know, pulled him out. I mean, we thought he might still be alive or something. What were we supposed to do, let him lie there?"

"And he was already dead when you pulled him out?"

"Y-yeah."

"Were you or your co-worker carrying anything in your hands at the time?" Deerhunter asked, his dark face unreadable.

The young man's face became frozen with confusion. "Wh-what do you mean?"

"Blunt objects. Hammers, shovels—"

"No! Do you think we— We just found him, that's all!"

"This is ridiculous," Jim muttered under his breath. He stepped toward the lieutenant. "Officer, is it necessary to harass this man? Can't you see how upset he is?"

"He's right," George said to Nancy.

"Uh-huh," Nancy replied, distracted by the sight of the old man talking to Red Sky Winsea at the edge of the crowd. "Can you stick around here a minute, George? I'll be right back."

Trying to blend in with the crowd, Nancy headed in the direction of the two Native Americans. Finally she was close enough so the old man's voice became clear above the din.

"I warned him," the man was saying. "I told him about the evil in this useless chunk of land, I told him not to stir the spirits up! But he just ignored me, laughed in my face."

"Yes, Grandfather," Sky answered. "But you were the one who leased him the land."

The old man stopped Sky with a sharp

glance. "And you know very well why I did. Besides, you remember what he said after we found out what he was doing—only a hole or two, that's all. He put on that little smile of his and said he'd leave if the spirits chased him out."

Sky nodded. "He didn't even have that chance."

For a moment Sky's and Nancy's eyes met. Nancy nodded briefly. She wound her way back through the crowd and found George in conversation with Jim.

After a few minutes she decided it was time to butt in. "Excuse me," she said, taking George's arm.

"What's going on?" George asked.

"We have to talk to Deerhunter," Nancy told her.

George turned to Jim, who was looking at them quizzically. "Nancy wants to—uh, ask the cops something. I guess she needs a little support."

Jim nodded vaguely. "Okay. See you later."

Nancy pulled George to a secluded area at the back of the tent. Making sure they were alone, she said, "I'm not sure, but I don't think the cave-in killed Dr. Langford."

"I don't get it, Nancy," George said. "We saw where Dr. Langford was taken out. He was buried alive."

"Not if the two volunteers could see him.

43

The collapse wasn't even bad enough to cover the entire floor of the trench, remember? There didn't seem to be enough weight to kill somebody as fit as Dr. Langford."

"So someone killed him, put him in the trench, then buried him in the avalanche?" George asked incredulously.

"The right idea, but the wrong order," Nancy said, catching a glimpse of Lieutenant Deerhunter by the tent entrance. He was a few steps away from the crowd, scribbling on his pad.

"You're getting weird on me," George protested. "I don't understand what you're—"

"Come with me," Nancy interrupted, walking past her.

They had to wait almost an hour to talk to Deerhunter. A polite but firm officer wouldn't let them near the lieutenant until he had finished all the various procedures.

When the two of them finally got to Deerhunter, he glanced up only briefly. "Uh-huh?"

"Excuse me, Lieutenant, may I talk to you?" Nancy asked.

"I have ears," the burly policeman said, without shifting his gaze to her.

"Well, I was just wondering if you've examined Dr. Langford's body for the cause of death."

Deerhunter stopped scribbling. He peered

up at Nancy from behind a pair of mirrored sunglasses. "Yes, we did, ma'am. Why?"

"It wasn't an accident, was it?" Nancy asked.

"Don't think so," the officer said. "Far as we can tell, the man was killed by a blow to the head."

"And the cave-in?" Nancy continued. "It was probably staged to cover up the murder, right?"

The officer took off his glasses, squinting at Nancy with cold, black eyes. "You sound like you know something about this, young lady. Want to tell me details?"

Nancy suddenly felt how close they were to the other people in the crowd. If she told him the truth, her secret would be out. "Uh, can we talk alone?"

"Yep." Deerhunter turned and peeked past the entrance flap of the tent. "Let's go in here."

He held open the flap, then followed Nancy and George inside. There was no one in the cluttered space, and the three of them followed the path through the pottery. Lieutenant Deerhunter found an empty area on top of Langford's folding table and sat there, facing Nancy. George sank into the canvas chair on the other side of the table, behind Deerhunter. Nancy stood in the middle of the room, facing them both.

"Lieutenant Deerhunter," Nancy said, "my

name is Nancy Drew and I'm a private detective, working undercover with my friend here, George Fayne."

A smile spread across Deerhunter's face. He glanced over his shoulder at George, then he looked back at Nancy and let out a deep guffaw.

"What's so funny?" George asked.

Deerhunter's potbelly shook as he laughed. When he stopped, his face became stern. "All right, girls—or, should I say, detectives? I have a lot of work to do, and—"

"Mr. Deerhunter, I'm serious," Nancy said. "Dr. Langford asked us to investigate some thefts at the site."

Deerhunter lifted himself off the desk and walked up to Nancy. "Miss Drew," he said, glowering down at her, "I am the investigating officer for this area, and for a good reason. I know my land, I know my people. There's a lot of police work to be done here—and police work is for the police. Am I understood?"

"Yes, sir," Nancy said quietly, looking away.

"Atta girl." He started to leave, then turned back around. "And if you do find any clues, I'd appreciate you telling me first, okay?"

With a quick smile and a wink, he left through the flap.

"What a jerk!" George said. She picked up a pen from the table and aimed it at the tent flap as if it were a dart.

"I think he's okay," Nancy said. "He just doesn't trust us—yet. What's wrong, George?"

George's eyes were glued to something on the table. Slowly she put the pen down. "Nancy," she said, picking up a wrinkled scrap of legal paper. "Look at this."

Nancy took it from her hand. There was a message made of cut-out letters from a newspaper pasted on it.

LEAVE THE DEAD ALONE,
OR JOIN THEM!

Chapter

Six

This sounds like somebody was out to get him," George said with a grimace.

"We've heard this threat before," Nancy mused. "Or something a lot like it."

"From Sky," George said as her mind flashed back. "The first time we saw her!"

Nancy nodded. "She seemed really serious about it, and just now I overheard her grandfather saying that *he'd* warned Dr. Langford not to mess with the evil spirits."

"Oh, so now we have a whole bunch of suspects," George commented.

"Sky, her grandfather, and who else?" Nancy asked.

George smiled. "The spirits."

The two of them laughed, but it sounded a little forced. Nancy couldn't help thinking of the horrendous-looking mask at the bottom of Vault One. After all the years it had been buried, it still seemed to bristle with life. Of course that didn't mean it *was* alive, she reasoned. But you never knew.

"Come on," she said. "We'd better hand over this clue to Lieutenant Deerhunter."

When they gave the note to Deerhunter, he scanned it impassively for a moment. Then, with a grunt, he turned and walked to his Jeep.

"You're welcome," George muttered to his back.

"Hey, guys?"

Nancy spun around at the sound of Frank Hardy's voice. "Huh?"

"Sorry," Frank said, walking up with Joe. "I didn't mean to startle you."

"Oh, no, you didn't," Nancy replied. "I was just—thinking about the case." She gestured and the four of them moved away from the crowd.

"We just heard what happened to Langford," Joe said. "It's awful."

Nancy exhaled. "I know."

"Things are pretty strange around here," George added. "What's happening with you guys?"

"We're ready to move in to the resort," Joe

answered, "and we can hang around to help you guys today, if you want, because our case is on hold for a day."

"We need to use the Altus library to do some research about the area, but it's closed on Mondays," Frank added.

"Just tell us what to do," Joe said.

Nancy thought a moment, then said, "Joe, remember Red Sky Winsea?"

Joe's face lit up. "Yes, I remember. Yes, I saw her right over there—and yes, I'll interview her."

"My brother, always one step ahead," Frank remarked.

"I'll let you know what happens," Joe said, turning to go.

As Joe headed off to the left, where Sky was beginning to walk away, the other three went right. There, a few yards away, solemn-faced volunteers were gathering around Dr. Ottman.

Everyone fell silent as Ottman began to speak. "This has been a sad, sad day," he announced. His heavy brow made a shadow that hid his eyes. "As Dr. Langford's second-in-command, I'll be taking charge of the dig. It's a duty I would once have coveted, but under these circumstances, I take it on with a heavy heart. Anyway, I'm in no condition to work, and I'm sure none of you is, either. So I'm suspending all activity at the site until tomorrow."

Murmurs rose from the crowd, but Ottman quieted them with a wave of his arm. "I ask all of you to keep your distance from the site today. The police are conducting an investigation there, and nothing is to be touched until they're finished." He mopped his balding pate, which glistened in the morning sun. "Tomorrow morning we'll meet at the site for work assignments—eight o'clock sharp. In the meantime, stay together and give each other support. Thank you."

As Ottman walked away, the crowd began to disperse. Nancy spotted a familiar figure approaching—Saul, the volunteer who had been with Frank the day before. There were three other diggers with him.

"Hi, guys," Saul said. He turned to his friends. "Sarah, Charlie, Heather—this is Nancy, George, and Frank."

"Hi," Nancy replied. She, Frank, and George fell in step with the others as they headed toward the resort.

"Too bad this had to happen after your first day," Saul said.

Nancy sighed. "Yeah. We didn't even get to know him."

"He seemed like a nice man, too," George commented.

Without saying anything, Saul raised his eyebrows slightly and gave his friends a strange glance.

"I guess he was," Heather said quickly. "I mean, he wasn't that bad to me."

"Yeah," Charlie added. "I don't think he deserved his rep."

"You mean, people didn't like him?" Frank prodded.

Saul rolled his eyes. "To put it mildly."

"Oh, come on, Saul, it wasn't like the guy was a monster or anything. He had a big ego, I guess," Charlie said to Frank. "The university people all used to talk behind his back. They said he got ahead in his field by taking credit for everyone else's work."

Heather chimed in, "There are all kinds of rumors. I heard he stole information from a Ph.D. candidate he was supervising and published it in a paper of his own."

"Yeah, and there was that Mayan dig years ago that put Langford on the map, academically—some incredible findings," Saul said. "Dr. Ottman was the head of the dig, and he was the up-and-coming expert on Mayan archaeology. Legend has it that Langford somehow stole the thunder from Ottman. I don't know any of the details, and I've heard Ottman laugh it off—"

"But Langford must have been pretty good," Nancy interjected. "I mean, this dig sounds like a real breakthrough."

Heather shrugged. "Well, we all heard that it

was really Jim Haber's work that led to the discovery of the Red Clay Vaults."

"But Jim seemed to really like Dr. Langford," George said. "Langford was his mentor."

"Langford was a charismatic guy," Heather replied. "He inspired loyalty. Maybe that's how he got away with this stuff."

There was an awkward silence. Their footsteps made muffled taps on the clay ground. Saul shook his head and frowned. "I don't know, guys, it's rotten to talk about him like this after he's gone. I mean, he's the reason we're all here."

The others guiltily mumbled their agreement. As they shuffled the last few yards to the resort, their conversation stopped. Nancy couldn't get Langford's face out of her mind. "There are still some important things to discuss" were the last words he had said to her.

It seemed that Nancy was going to have to find out what those important things were by herself.

The thermometer outside the resort kitchen had peaked over the hundred-degree mark as Nancy, George, and Frank carried their lunch trays inside early that afternoon.

"Wow," George said, gesturing at the thermometer. "What are we going to do now, sleuth around until we fry?"

"What else is there to do around here?" Frank asked. "We could try to track down Joe, but I have a feeling he may not want to be tracked."

Nancy's blue eyes glinted. "Well, there's always Lake Altus—"

"Now we're talking!" George exclaimed with a grin.

"I'll meet you in front of the main building," Frank said, and he ran off to his room in the west wing of the three-story, rambling resort building.

Nancy and George's room was in the opposite direction. They went through the east wing's entrance, letting the blast of air-conditioning send a pleasant shock through their bodies. They took the stairs two at a time to the second floor.

George was the first into the room. She pulled her duffel bag off the floor and threw it on her bed. As she rummaged through it, Nancy opened the top drawer of her dresser.

Nancy tried to decide between a new orange French-cut bathing suit, and an older, slightly less daring model. She stared at them both, indecisive. "George?" she said, still peering at the suits. "Do you think I should—"

"YEEEEEEEEAAAAAAHH!"

George's scream made Nancy jump. She spun around to see George standing stock-still, staring at her duffel bag.

Coiled in the bag, its tail buzzing angrily, was a huge, hissing rattlesnake!

Chapter

Seven

THE SNAKE WRIGGLED onto the bed and dropped to the floor, inches from George's feet.

George was still frozen in place. She couldn't even scream now.

"George, move!" Nancy shouted. Whirling around, she grabbed a beach towel from the top of her dresser. She flung it over the snake, covering it completely.

Continuing the motion, she wrapped her arms around George and yanked her back. The two girls fell onto the floor. Beside them, the towel undulated furiously.

With an angry *sssssss*, the snake suddenly

peered out from under the towel. Nancy and George sprang to their feet.

"What the—"

The new voice in the room was Jim's. He quickly took a wastebasket from beside Nancy's dresser. In a swift shoveling motion, he scooped the snake into the basket and pushed the towel in after it.

"Jim, be careful!" George shouted.

Jim held the basket by the bottom, extending it as far away from his body as he could. As he backed out the door, Nancy slipped ahead of him and ran down the hallway. She pushed open the back exit, letting Jim race through, with George close behind.

The three of them rushed down the stairs and out the rear exit. They were bombarded by the searing heat as they ran across the back parking lot. At the edge, in a thick patch of scrub brush, Jim stopped. He turned the wastebasket over, and the rattlesnake tumbled out in a tangle of beach towel.

From a safe distance, the three of them watched the snake slither out and disappear into the brush, its coils writhing in a curious sideways motion.

Jim grabbed the towel and shook it out. "I don't want the resort to accuse you of stealing," he said with a relieved smile.

"How did that—thing get in my bag?" George asked, still wide-eyed with shock.

"He wanted to escape the heat, I guess," Jim replied. "It happens sometimes. I have to tell you, that's the biggest sidewinder I've seen in a long time."

"Thanks for helping us," Nancy said.

Jim shrugged. "Hey, no problem. I'm just glad I heard George's scream."

They began walking back to the hotel. "We were about to get changed and go to the lake," George said. "Now I'm not sure I want to go back into the room."

Jim laughed. "Make sure you check the sink drain."

George stopped in her tracks. "You don't really mean they—"

"Just kidding!" Jim said. "Don't worry too much, you guys. If you need any heroics, I'll be in my room, okay?"

"You sure you don't want to come with us?" George asked.

"Can't," Jim answered. "I have work to do, and there's a meeting this afternoon about divvying up Tod's work. Till then I'll be in my room, three-fifty-one, if you need me. See you!"

As he turned to go, Nancy and George went in through the rear door. Climbing up the stairs, George shuddered. "That was awful. I can't believe how lucky we were."

"I can't, either," Nancy said, deep in thought.

"Uh-oh. That's your I'm-suspicious tone of voice. What's up, Nancy?"

"Well, it seems funny to me that Jim just happened to come by when we found that snake. His room is in the other wing."

"Maybe he was coming to see me—er, us."

"He never said that, though. He never gave us any reason." Nancy pushed through the second-floor door and stepped into the hallway. "Maybe he knew about the snake. Maybe it was planted."

"That's ridiculous!" George protested. "Why on earth would he put a rattlesnake in my duffel bag?"

"Maybe he—or whoever did it—was trying to scare *me,* not you." Nancy went straight to their room and picked the bag off the bed. Holding it up, she thrust the name tag toward George.

George jumped back. "Hey, easy! What if there's another surprise in there?"

"There isn't," Nancy said. "Except maybe for the name on the duffel bag—the duffel bag you borrowed from me, remember?"

"'Nancy Drew,'" George read. "Someone could have assumed it was your bag!"

"Could be. I've started making a few waves around here, so our culprit might be taking notice. And if he's sneaky enough to get away with vandalism and murder, who knows what else he'd do?"

George snapped her fingers, suddenly looking pleased with herself. "Well, it couldn't have been Jim! He knew I was using your bag—we told him at the airport."

Nancy admired her friend. "You're right. I had forgotten that. I guess there's still an off-chance that he could have done it, but it does seem fairly unlikely."

They both turned around at a hollow rapping sound on their door. Frank was there, peering in with an expression of disbelief. Behind him were four volunteers who were staying on the same floor as Nancy and George. "Hey, I know girls are supposed to take longer than guys to get ready," Frank said, "but this is ridiculous—"

George arched an eyebrow. "Frank Hardy, you will not stereotype us!"

"We had a crisis," Nancy said. "There was a rattlesnake in George's duffel bag."

Frank stared at her curiously for a moment. When he realized she was serious, he pursed his lips in a silent whistle. "Well, I guess that's a good enough excuse," he said.

"So that's what the noise was all about," one of the other volunteers added. "All that screaming and chasing through the halls."

"Just two helpless females and the brave male who saved them," George said dryly.

"You didn't happen to see anybody come

into this room before we got here, did you?" Nancy asked the girls in the hallway. "Or anyone suspicious lurking around?"

All of them shook their heads. A dark, short-haired girl spoke up. "But anyone could have sneaked in when we went outside to hear the news about Dr. Langford. This whole wing was empty for a couple of hours."

One of the others, a tall, redheaded girl, added, "Someone could have hauled in a nuclear bomb and no one would have noticed."

Nancy nodded. Out of the corner of her eye, she saw Frank blanch. She knew he was making an uncomfortable connection with his own case.

Even though she knew the statement wasn't serious, she felt the hairs on the back of her neck slowly start to rise.

Joe's rented car bounced over a rutted road as it approached a cluster of ramshackle houses. "This is it?" he asked.

Red Sky Winsea held on to the dashboard as the car jolted over a deep hole. "You were expecting Bayport, New York?"

Joe shot her a startled glance. "How did you know that's where I come from?"

"You told me," Sky replied. "At least twice."

"Oh, sorry," Joe said with an embarrassed

smile. "I guess I've been doing a lot of talking."

"It's all right," Sky said. "I've enjoyed your company and I appreciate the ride."

"I enjoyed the tour." Sky had given Joe a short tour of the area. "I couldn't believe you were actually going to walk all the way home."

"I begin each day with a long walk, sometimes I go to the dig site. Keeps me in shape for my job."

"Which is?" Joe asked. She was warming up to him, he could tell.

"A waitress at the Silver Lounge. It takes a lot of stamina to tote steaks all night. There's my house, on the left." She pointed out the window at a one-story stucco house. Behind it was a fenced-in pasture where two horses were grazing on tough, brownish grass.

Joe pulled into the dirt yard in front of her door and stopped. "What a trip!" he said amiably. "This car's going to need a new pair of shocks!"

"Yes," Sky answered. She pushed the door open and got out. "Thanks again."

No invitation. Joe realized he was going to have to think fast. "Uh, you wouldn't happen to have a soda or something? I'm pretty dehydrated."

Sky smiled. "Sure. Would you like to come in?"

"Why not?" Getting out of the car, Joe fought back a triumphant grin. He followed Sky through the front door and into a small living room, crammed with small tables and bookshelves. Statuettes and pottery decorated the tables and served as bookends on the shelves. Indian jewelry and knickknacks were draped over table edges and lined up along the top of an old television. In the center of the room was a sofa festooned with faded throw pillows, one of which was embroidered with an Oklahoma University insignia. The others bore printed designs that looked American Indian.

"Grandfather? Are you here?" Sky called out. She waited for a moment, then said, "He must not be back yet. Make yourself at home." She switched on an electric fan, then walked into the small kitchen that adjoined the living room.

"Are you a student?" Joe asked, picking up the embroidered pillow.

"A junior," Sky called over her shoulder.

"You didn't tell me that."

"You didn't ask."

Joe wandered over to one of the bookshelves. "Nice place," he said. He picked up a clay pot and stared at the faded figure painted on it. A sinister lizard-tongued face glared at him. "Not a friendly guy, huh?"

"I got that on a trip out east," Sky said. "It's an evil spirit from a place called Manchonake, which means 'Island of Death' in the tongue of the Montauk tribe."

"Oh." Joe quickly put it back. "Sorry, pal, just passing through."

Sky chuckled as she opened the refrigerator. "Cola all right?"

"Perfect," Joe replied. His eyes glanced from shelf to shelf, taking in the rest of the pottery, some of which was glued together from pieces. "Is this stuff from around here?"

"Sure," Sky answered. "Some of it has been passed down from my tribal ancestors. Some of it I buy, if I'm sure it's been obtained lawfully. Some of it I find."

"Mm-hm." Joe picked up an ornate gold necklace and let its medallions dangle between his fingers. "Valuable stuff, too. Don't you worry about thieves?"

Sky came back into the living room, carrying two glasses filled with cola and ice. "Why? Are you interested in becoming one?" she asked with a sly smile.

Joe noticed the way her hair shimmered like the blackest silk. Her smile was strong and dazzling, with perfect white teeth set off by the dark reddish hue of her skin. As she held out a glass to Joe, her glance took hold of him. She was crazy about him—Joe was sure of it.

Joe took the glass and gently swirled the soda around so the ice cubes clinked. "A thief? Me? Hey, you don't get much more honest than Joe Hardy."

"Oh?" Sky said, sitting in an armchair. "Can you honestly tell me what you're doing at the site? You don't seem like the archaeologist type."

"I guess I'm just full of surprises," Joe said with a modest laugh. He plopped himself into the sofa and sank comfortably into the cushions. "How about you? What's your interest in the site? You seem to spend a lot of time out there."

"My only interest is to stand up for justice," Sky replied, her jaw set determinedly. "No one has the right to disturb the dead. The graves should be filled in and left alone."

"Well, after what's been happening there, it looks like somebody else agrees with you."

"Or something," Sky said.

"Oh, come on, you don't really believe that ghosts came out of the dirt and killed Dr. Langford. That's crazy!"

"For hundreds of years the Red Clay People believed in those spirits. Were they all crazy?"

"I'm sorry," Joe said. "I don't mean any disrespect." He took another swig of soda. Sky's pottery, her talk of evil spirits, her frank questions were all making him think about

Nancy's case. For the first time that day he looked at her as a suspect. "I just can't help thinking someone's been sneaking in the site late at night. I mean, somebody could wander over there on a midnight drive."

"Joe, I believe the legends," she finally said. "That's all. If you're going to try to convert me, you're wasting your breath. People make fun of me all the time at the university. I'm used to people like you."

Joe chugged the last of his soda. Sky's eyes were distant now, icy. It was fast dawning on him that he had an uphill climb—on more than one count.

When Joe arrived at the lake, it was three o'clock. The sun was beginning to cast deep shadows on the nearby hills, and the water was a calm, rich blue green. There were at least a dozen volunteers sunbathing and swimming. Joe spotted Frank, Nancy, and George sitting on a small wooden dock. A bright red windsurfboard rested on the ground a few feet from them.

Just my luck to get here after the wind died down, Joe said to himself. He was in a bad mood.

"Hi, Joe!" George called out, waving to him. Joe waved back silently.

"Well?" Nancy said as he walked up to them.

Joe shrugged. "No luck. All I could find out from her is that she believes in ghosts."

"That's all you talked about all that time?" Frank asked, raising an eyebrow.

"How about you?" Joe retorted, sounding harsher than he meant to. "What great developments did I miss?"

He listened skeptically as Frank filled him in on the snake episode. Then Nancy spoke up.

"We found a few things out from some of the diggers here at the lake. Sky's grandfather, the guy we saw this morning, leased this land to Oklahoma University in exchange for free tuition for Sky."

Joe frowned. "She didn't tell me that."

"You probably didn't ask," Frank remarked.

"Apparently he—his name is John Whiteshirt—thought it was a great deal," Nancy went on. "The land was worthless to him. He couldn't sell it because it was against the wishes of his father, who left it to him in a will. But Whiteshirt couldn't afford the taxes on the land. At the same time Sky was having a hard time paying her college tuition. Both her parents had died and Whiteshirt was her guardian, so he felt he had to help her come up with the money somehow."

"He had been complaining to the locals that the land was cursed because it wasn't good enough to farm," Frank said, taking up the story. "So the university's offer took him completely by surprise. And when they agreed to throw in Sky's tuition, as well as take over the tax payments, he jumped at the chance."

"He didn't know about the Red Clay People site?" Joe asked.

"No one did, until Langford found it," Nancy said. "And then Whiteshirt had a fit when they started digging."

"How did you find all this out?" Joe asked.

"Langford used to talk about it to his students," Frank answered. "They all knew about it."

Joe sat on the dock and stared across the lake. "So Sky and Whiteshirt were both angry at Langford for digging up the graves."

"But they had to let him, because they're both in debt to the university," Nancy said. "Sky for her tuition, Whiteshirt for his taxes."

"And a rattlesnake just happens to show up in a duffel bag," Joe added, still sorting things out. "Maybe put there by Jim Haber, maybe by those pesky evil spirits."

Having remained silent for a while, George finally spoke up. "I think there's only one thing to do," she said, poising herself for a dive off the dock.

Everyone looked her way. "What's that?" Nancy asked.

"Visit the spirits tonight!" George said, then she plunged into the water.

* * *

The light from the full moon, low and swollen, was almost bright enough to blot out the stars that night. But as Nancy, George, Frank, and Joe climbed over the yellow Police —Off Limits tapes placed around Red Clay Vault Thirteen, the moonglow only made things worse. Its dull radiance seemed to give every shadow life. As they climbed down into the trench, George whispered, "I'm glad this isn't the vault where that eagle mask was, Nan."

Nancy gave a nervous laugh. "Me, too!"

Shining his flashlight ahead of him, Frank checked the pile of red dirt from the cave-in. Some of it had been dug out so he had a clean passage to the far side away from the others. He felt a chill—the night was quite cool. Now, far from the others, he was beginning to hear noises. Rustling, shuffling.

Only some tumbleweeds, or a nocturnal lizard, he told himself. No need to climb back out and look.

Scritch—scritch—scritch—hmmm—

He could swear he heard a guttural kind of hum that time, a growl or purr maybe. He couldn't ignore this.

He raised his eyes to the rim of the trench, shutting off his flashlight so the beam wouldn't be seen.

Something was there. Silhouetted in the moonlight. Swaying back and forth. It was the size of a human, with arms and legs like a human.

Suddenly it moved toward the lip of the trench. Frank saw it more clearly, and a gasp caught in his throat. His flashlight clattered to the ground.

The thing was covered with fur from head to toe. It lifted its head, and Frank could see a snout, long and sharp like a wolf's. The thing's razorlike teeth caught the glint of the moon as it turned its head.

And then it was staring right into Frank's eyes.

Chapter

Eight

Uh—GUYS?" Frank said, the words catching in his throat. "Guys? Come here!"

Running footsteps slapped against the hard clay floor. The others emerged from the shadow of the trench's remaining erect wall.

"What is it, Frank?" Nancy called softly.

Frank cringed as her flashlight glare caught him in the eye. "Up there!" He pointed toward the edge of the trench.

The moon was low to the horizon, its outline interrupted only by a tall cactus plant.

"Hey, pretty scary, Frank," Joe said. "The branches sort of look like arms."

Frank squinted, trying to make out any movement in the darkness surrounding the moon. "There was something there," he insisted. "I know it sounds crazy, but it was some kind of creature—half-wolf, half-human. I saw it. I even heard it growling!"

"Hey, I heard growling, too!" George chimed in. "I thought it was some—I don't know, prairie dog or something."

"Prairie dogs chatter," Joe corrected.

"Are you sure it wasn't a wolf, a coyote?" Nancy asked Frank.

"Standing upright, with hands and fingers?" Frank said. He immediately began climbing the trench. "Come on!"

They all scrabbled up the sloping side that had caved in, but when they got to the top, they saw nothing. Only the black holes of the other trenches, which looked like inkblots on the moonlit sheen of the Oklahoma clay.

"Oh, brother," George groaned as she looked in the mirror the next morning. "Who are *you?*"

"What's the matter?" Nancy called out from the bedroom. "Not enough sleep?"

"I don't know if I got to sleep," George called back. "We should never have gone to the site last night."

"Yeah, it bothered me, too," Nancy admitted.

"What if that thing was a werewolf? Now, don't laugh at me, Nancy; I mean, it was *Frank* who saw it, not some wacko."

"I'm not laughing," Nancy answered.

George ran a comb through her dark hair and stepped into the bedroom. "Maybe when we get outside it won't seem so creepy." She grabbed a pair of jeans and stepped into them. Then she turned to her dresser and frowned. "Where's my wallet?"

"Beats me," Nancy replied. "Did you have it last night?"

"I don't know." George began rummaging through her drawers, then looked inside her duffel bag. "Oh, great. It was leather—what if the rattlesnake ate it, thinking it was some strange domestic pet?"

Nancy smiled. "I wonder if snakes can digest snapshots."

"It's not that funny, Nan. Maybe it was stolen."

"I know. You should probably file a report."

George looked at her watch. "Yeah, later. We're due at the site in ten minutes—and Dr. Ottman seems like the kind of guy who eats people for lunch if they're late."

Nancy thought of Ottman's stern, scowling face and suddenly began to hurry. This was not the time to get on the wrong side of the people in charge.

* * *

Frank exhaled, frustrated. He closed a newspaper, folded it, and stuck it on top of the pile that was growing in front of him.

"Anything yet?" came Joe's voice behind him.

"Shhh," Frank admonished, turning around. "This is a library!"

"Oh, I hadn't noticed," Joe said in a stage whisper. He pulled up a blond-wood chair, which scraped on the linoleum floor of the Altus public library. The librarian, a thin, elderly woman with a beehive hairdo who sat at a nearby desk, stared at Joe over the top of her glasses.

"Did you get through to the air force base?" Frank asked softly.

"Yes, sir!" Joe answered with a little salute. "I set up an appointment to talk to Captain Van Allen Lorimor. He was in charge of the checkpoint our trucks supposedly went through."

"Van Allen Lorimor?"

"I know. Sounds like a movie company or something. How about you? Anything in the papers?"

"Not about the trucks," Frank said, sifting through the rumpled pile. "The only article about any truck accident was some local pickup that skidded into a chicken coop."

"'Radioactive omelets discovered in rural

Oklahoma—news at eleven!'" Joe intoned in a TV newscaster's voice.

"I did find something interesting," Frank said. "I came across it just by accident, but it might be useful." He pulled out one of the papers and opened it to a page near the back. There was a small, fuzzy photo of Sky and a bald man in a conservative suit, standing together in what looked like a courtroom. Above the photo was the headline "Comanches Denied Stop Order for Dig."

"It says here that Whiteshirt and Sky tried to have the dig declared illegal under tribal law," Frank said. "The guy in the picture is a lawyer named Gregory Fripp, a half-blood Comanche. He works in a small firm in Altus; I wrote down all the details."

Joe leaned forward, his blue eyes bright with mischief. "Sounds like someone who might be able to give Nancy information about *her* case. Frank, are you sure you aren't still carrying a torch for Nancy? You're doing all her work for her."

Frank ignored the comment and reached into his pocket for change. "I'll call her."

Joe sighed. "Frank, she's probably at the dig, and besides, our meeting is at ten-thirty. From the sound of Captain Lorimor, we'd better not show up late."

Frank looked at his watch. "That's only a

half hour from now. How long does it take to get there?"

"Close to a half hour."

Frank whisked the newspapers off the table and stuffed them into their place on a nearby shelf. He could hear the librarian cluck disapprovingly at him and Joe as they raced out the door.

They ran to the parking lot, hopped into the car, and pulled away with a squeal of tires.

As Frank and Joe wound their way through Altus, they could hear the roar of military transport planes overhead. Jackson Air Force Base was outside town, just off the main highway. Fifteen minutes after they started they turned around and looked behind them. It was hard to remember they'd just come from a town. Altus had no suburbs. It just ended, and the hot, parched plain took over, stretching endlessly along the horizon.

Joe was driving. Frank stared out the window at the dry landscape, thinking about what Joe had said in the library. He *had* once been pretty attracted to Nancy, and she had liked him, too, but they had gotten over that. They had decided it was better if they were just friends.

And they were *good* friends. Frank had never met anyone whose thoughts about crime solving were so much in sync with his own.

Nancy was a kindred spirit. Frank suspected Joe teased him about the pretty red-haired detective because Joe felt a little left out when the three of them got together.

"We're coming up on the base," Joe announced.

Pulling out of his own thoughts, Frank glanced at his watch. "Right on schedule," he declared.

At ten twenty-two the Hardys pulled up to the guard gate at the base. After confirming their names and handing them ID tags, the guard gave them directions.

They barreled across the base, detouring around a network of long runways. At ten twenty-seven, they screeched to a halt in the parking lot outside Captain Lorimor's building and ran inside to the reception desk. "Captain Lorimor, please," Joe gasped. "We're Frank and Joe Hardy."

Behind the desk, a tan, blond-haired woman in a crisp military uniform smiled at him and picked up her phone. "Cutting it close, aren't you?" she said.

"Well, I just talked to him—" Joe began.

"Captain Lorimor?" the woman said into the phone. "They've arrived, sir. Yes, sir." She hung up and told the boys, "Please take a seat."

Frank and Joe sank into an uncomfortable

olive green vinyl sofa. Several air force officials passed through the hallway behind the desk, walking briskly with ramrod-straight postures. Their uniforms were neatly pressed and their military-issue black shoes gleamed with the reflection of fluorescent lights overhead.

Joe fidgeted, tucking his Bayport Slop Shop T-shirt into his jeans. "I can see we're really going to go over big."

At ten forty-nine the receptionist answered a buzz on her intercom. "Yes, sir. All right, sir." She turned to Frank and Joe. "You can go on in. It's the first door on your left."

The brothers followed her instructions and knocked on Lorimor's door. "Come in!" a deep, throaty voice barked.

Joe pushed the door open. "Hello, Captain Lorimor."

As he and Frank stepped in, Lorimor turned away from a large window that looked out on the airstrips. The first thing Frank noticed was his medals—dozens of them lined up above his jacket pocket. He had a head of thick hair, graying at the temples and cut in a short military style. His blue-gray eyes were like lasers, piercing and hard. Veins throbbed in his neck, and the taut, red skin of his face made him look as if he were on the verge of exploding with anger. Frank guessed that he always looked that way.

"Where are the Network fellas?" Lorimor asked in a gruff voice that was just below a shout.

"Uh, we are them—they," Joe replied.

"You two?" Lorimor said, his eyes flashing with astonishment. "This isn't some high school prank, is it? Because if it is—"

"No, sir," Frank said. "We're Frank and Joe Hardy. I'm sure if you checked your list of Network operatives—"

Lorimor slapped his pencil on his desk and shook his head. "What kind of agency is this Network?" he growled. "I'm supposed to trust matters of national security to a couple of Boy Scouts?"

"I'm sorry, sir," Frank answered, "but—"

"Don't be sorry," Lorimor shot back. "This is typical of the whole government these days. They consider us a second-class organization . . . obsolete!" He pointed out his office window. "You see those runways over there? You could fit a small city on each of them. They were built to accommodate the NZE-809, the world's largest jet. Now what are they doing? Growing weeds! You see those hangars, the size of football fields? They were supposed to house a fleet of new fighter jets, but production on the fleet was canceled. Why? Cutbacks in military spending. Suddenly the most advanced military hardware is unnecessary!

What's going to be their excuse when the United States has to crawl on its belly to some second-rate gang of nuclear terrorists?"

Frank and Joe nodded politely and waited for him to finish. Finally Joe spoke up. "Uh, Captain Lorimor, sir . . . if you could just give us the information I requested over the phone—"

Lorimor rummaged through a pile of papers on his desk and drew out a photocopied list. Pointing to a meaningless jumble of numbers near the top, he pushed the paper toward Frank and Joe. "There's the record of the shipments. I checked them through myself."

Joe looked at the paper uncomprehendingly. "The drivers didn't say anything about a detour, or engine trouble, or anything unusual?"

"They checked through," Lorimor said, drumming his fingers on the desk. "That's all I know."

"Nothing about—" Frank began.

"Son, I said that's all I know!" Lorimor snapped back. "In the air force, boys, we do not repeat ourselves."

"Right," Frank said, adding a quick *sir* as he and Joe turned to leave.

"If I can be of any further help," Lorimor said, "don't hesitate to call."

Frank fought the urge to laugh. "Yes, thank you, sir," he said. He and Joe walked into the hallway, closing the door behind them.

"So glad we rushed to get here," Joe remarked. "What now?"

Frank shrugged. "Up to Quartz Mountain, I guess. We may be back to square one, but at least we can tell Nancy about the article we saw."

As they passed the receptionist, Joe said, "Thank you, we had a lovely time." He was answered by a blank look.

Stepping out into the oppressive heat, Frank and Joe both breathed sighs of relief.

At the dig site George followed Nancy along the edge of Red Clay Vault Thirteen. "I don't see anything," George said, checking nervously over her shoulder. "Besides, what do wolf tracks look like, anyway?"

"We'll know them when we see them," Nancy answered. She crouched down to look at some prints, but they were definitely human. Smooth-soled, like those made by moccasins. Probably by one of the volunteers.

"Yeah, well, we don't, so I think we should get back to the place Ottman assigned us. He's mean, Nancy. You saw the way he looked at us when we showed up two minutes late this morning—" She stopped abruptly. "Uh-oh!"

Nancy looked up. "What?"

"I knew we shouldn't have wandered off," George said. "He sent the cops after us!"

Walking toward them was Lieutenant

Deerhunter, his jaw set firmly. Nancy and George watched as he reached for something in his pocket.

"He's going to shoot us," George said. "Should we put our hands in the air?"

"Stop it, George!" Nancy said. Then she called out, "What can we do for you, officer?"

"Searching for something?" he asked, staring pointedly at George.

"Well, uh—" George began.

Deerhunter pulled a small, rectangular, brown object out of his pocket. "Maybe I can help. This belong to you?"

George stared at her wallet, nestled in Deerhunter's fleshy right palm. "Yes! Where did you find it?"

"I didn't," he said. "One of the volunteers spotted it. This morning, right here in Vault Thirteen. I'm surprised we missed it yesterday."

As George stood there, frozen, Deerhunter flipped her the wallet and said, "Come along. I'm taking you in for questioning on the murder of Tod Langford."

Chapter

Nine

Hᴇʏ, ᴡᴀɪᴛ ᴀ ᴍɪɴᴜᴛᴇ," George said. "I didn't kill Langford!"

"Follow me," Deerhunter said, turning away.

"The reason you didn't find the wallet yesterday was because it wasn't there! I must have dropped it last night—" George tried to cut herself off, but it was too late.

Deerhunter slowly swiveled his head to glance over his shoulder. "Oh? And what were you doing in the trench—the trench that I sealed off to all unauthorized personnel—last night?"

George appealed frantically to Nancy with her eyes. "Well, er, I—I—"

"Can I come with you, lieutenant?" Nancy asked calmly. "I'm involved, too."

"The more the merrier," Deerhunter said. He led them to his Jeep, parked at the edge of the site. As they climbed in, the volunteers nearby watched with curiosity. A few yards away Ottman stood with a delicate brush in his hand. In the heat he had unbent so far as to remove his khaki shirt and the tangle of objects he usually wore around his neck. He glanced at Deerhunter impassively before returning to his work.

Deerhunter drove around the ridge to the headquarters tent. "I'm using this as my headquarters for the investigation. We'll be nice and private in here, like last time," he said.

Sure enough, no one else was in the tent. It was also about ten degrees cooler, and Nancy felt a sudden chill.

"So," Deerhunter said, pacing the narrow pathway between the piles of potsherds, "would you care to tell me about the wallet?"

"Officer, I'm not the murderer," George said. "I—we—Nancy and I were just exploring Vault Thirteen last night, that's all. Looking for clues—"

"Clues?" Deerhunter raised an eyebrow.

"We didn't do any harm, lieutenant," Nancy said. "If George had dropped her wallet the night Langford was killed, your men would have found it yesterday morning."

Deerhunter nodded. He turned to face Nancy squarely. "I don't really suspect your friend of murdering Langford. As soon as I saw the wallet I figured she was there last night."

Nancy could see George's shoulders loosen, as if a huge weight had been lifted. "Well, I can assure you we didn't vandalize the vault, either," Nancy said. "If you check the inventory—"

"I don't have to check," Deerhunter replied. "I don't believe you're crooks, either. But what I do believe is that you girls know more than you're telling. And I have a feeling you're going to continue sneaking around investigating, no matter what I say."

Nancy's eyes shifted from Deerhunter to the floor.

"Don't worry," the lieutenant said with a half smile. "I'm not going to ask you to stop."

"You're not?" Nancy asked disbelievingly.

"No. I've decided that would be foolish. I am going to ask you to cooperate, though." He reached into his left pocket and pulled out a small gold medallion, mounted to be hung on a necklace. "This was in Langford's hand when he died."

He gave it to Nancy. She and George examined its strange, angular carvings.

"According to Dr. Ottman, it's a Red Clay

People artifact," Deerhunter said. "But it doesn't match any of the other items in Vault Thirteen. We think it was taken from another vault."

"By Dr. Langford?" George asked.

"Possibly," Deerhunter answered. "But in my opinion, not likely. I think he may have grabbed it from his killer in the struggle."

"Which means his killer and the thief may be the same person," Nancy added.

"It's a good guess," Deerhunter said. He folded his arms. "Okay, I've told you what I know. Now you tell me what you know."

Nancy took a deep breath. With Deerhunter's massive frame looming over her in the tent, she felt claustrophobic. Her eyes passed over the piles of potsherds, the magnifying glass, and pencil jar Langford had left on his desk. A strange little box with dials and gauges sat under the corner of the table. She stared blankly at the box, which looked somehow familiar, as she put together the words she would say to Deerhunter. Finally she began to speak and unravel the events of the last two days. The conversations with Langford, the statements of Whiteshirt and Sky, the snake in the duffel bag, the late-night trip to the vault all came out. She even told Deerhunter about Frank and Joe, though she kept the Hardys' real mission to herself.

Deerhunter took it all in, and when she

stopped, he asked, "Is that it? You're not leaving out anything?"

"That's it," Nancy said. "Give us a few days and we'll have more."

"Fair enough," Deerhunter replied. He began walking to the door. "Keep me posted, that's all I ask."

"You bet," George said, looking gratefully at him.

As they were walking out, a car came to a quick stop outside the tent, spewing up red dust.

Frank and Joe hopped out of opposite doors. "Hope we're not interrupting anything," Joe said.

"No," answered Deerhunter laconically. He got into his car and started up. "Oh, by the way—thank you, boys," he called out.

As he pulled away, Joe turned to Nancy. "What was that all about? Thank us for what?"

Nancy grinned at him and Frank. "For your promise to assist and cooperate with the police," she told them.

"You told him everything?" asked Frank, embarrassed. Joe let out a laugh.

"Everything except the werewolf," George said. "Don't worry, your secret is safe with us."

"Well, I didn't want him to think we were out of our minds," Nancy said, grinning at Frank. "How's your case going?"

"Not so terrific," Frank answered. "But we may have a lead for you. A lawyer named Greg Fripp represented Sky and her grandfather in a suit against Oklahoma University. They lost the case, but I'm sure Fripp might be able to give you some info."

"Great!" Nancy said. "Where's his office?"

"In Altus," Frank replied. "I'll drive you."

"Hey, wait a second," George interrupted. "I don't think Dr. Ottman's going to be very happy about two of his staff taking the whole morning off. Maybe we should wait till later."

"After five, Fripp won't be in his office," Frank pointed out.

"I'll go back to the dig with George and take Nancy's place," Joe suggested. "I'm not Nancy, but all he wants is a pair of strong hands anyway."

"Thanks, Joe," Frank said. "We'll try to meet you guys back here during the afternoon break. Where will you be?"

Joe shrugged and looked at George. "The lake?"

George nodded enthusiastically.

"Okay, see you." Frank and Nancy got into the car as George and Joe walked toward the dig site. Traffic was light, and they got to Altus in fifteen minutes. Frank reached into his pocket and took out the information he had written down. By asking a few people on the street, he and Nancy were able to find the Altus

Professional Building, which contained Fripp's office.

It was a three-story clapboard building wedged between a movie theater and an automobile showroom. When they walked through the front door, a harried, gum-chewing receptionist pointed them to the back of a warren of small offices that stretched down a narrow hallway. Fripp's was the last one, just beyond the broom closet.

As Nancy walked there, she had only the vaguest idea of what she would ask Fripp. One thing was certain: she and Frank had to get him to talk about the case. Something useful was bound to spill out.

"Mr. Fripp?" Nancy called out, looking into his office.

A small, trim, middle-aged man with sharp features and bloodshot eyes peered up from the desk. Droplets of perspiration glistened at the edges of his receding hairline, and his rep tie hung loosely from an unbuttoned collar. "Yes?" he asked.

"My name is Nancy Drew, and this is Frank Hardy. We're friends of Red Sky Winsea and John Whiteshirt."

Fripp sat back in his worn leather armchair. His harried expression softened. "Ah, two classmates of Sky's, eh? Looking for some career advice? Have a seat!" He gestured toward two metal chairs opposite the desk.

"Well, we're not actually—" Nancy started to say.

"I've known Sky since she was knee-high to a prairie dog, you know," Fripp rattled on as Frank and Nancy sat. "Her old granddaddy was like a father to me. Well, actually more like an uncle. I'd hate to have a crazy old coot like that for a dad, you know what I mean?"

"He's a wild one, isn't he?" said Frank cautiously.

Fripp laughed. "Nuts. Completely bonkers. I don't know how the girl puts up with him. I don't know how *I* put up with representing him!"

"We heard about your case," Nancy said. "Too bad."

"Hey, that's life in the big leagues," Fripp said with a shrug. "They didn't have a chance of winning that suit against Oklahoma U. Tribal law doesn't apply to Whiteshirt's land, since it's privately owned and not part of the reservation. But who am I to turn down a job? Anyway, I owed Whiteshirt a favor or two. You know, the old man is obsessed with that god-forsaken land of his."

"It's a beautiful area," Nancy said.

"Between you and me, it's a piece of junk," Fripp said. "You know, years ago, when I was just out of college, he took me and a bunch of other kids wildcatting on that land. We were convinced we were going to strike gushers of oil and retire on the spot. When we didn't find anything, he took it hard. Then a few years later he started getting into this stuff about evil spirits in the land."

"What made you look for oil there?" Nancy asked.

Fripp leaned back, as if he were about to go into a long story. "Well, in this neck of the woods, you——"

The electronic chirp of a phone cut him off. "Excuse me," he said, sitting forward and picking up the receiver. "Fripp here. Yep— that's right. . . ."

As he talked on, Frank sneaked a look at Nancy. The conversation so far was promising. Was Whiteshirt crazy enough to mastermind the murder, the vandalism, the thefts? Was he afraid of someone finding oil during the dig? What were Fripp's thoughts about the case?

Nancy was dying to ask more questions as Fripp continued mumbling into the phone: "Mm-hm . . . Oh? . . . Right away . . . You bet . . . 'Bye now."

He hung up the phone and stood up. "Looks like I'm popular today. Listen, kids, we'll have to continue this another time, okay?"

"But we just——" Frank began to protest.

"Just give me a little advance warning, and we'll set up an appointment." Fripp came around his desk and began ushering the two of them out. "It was a pleasure. See you soon, and say hi to Sky for me."

Before they knew it, Frank and Nancy were in the hallway, with a closed door inches from their faces.

When Nancy saw the glum expression on Frank's lean features, she had to smile. "You look exactly like I feel," she told him. "Come on, let's get a soda—my treat. And then we'll go back to the lake for a swim."

"Hey, big spender," Frank teased as they walked out to the car. "A guy could go far with you."

Nancy's blue eyes sparkled with amusement. "You bet," she said, and squeezed Frank's arm affectionately. "You bet."

Almost an hour later, at Lake Altus, George was telling Joe what had happened with Lieutenant Deerhunter earlier. "He took me in for questioning. I thought he was accusing me of killing Dr. Langford, but he just wanted our help. I think he's actually an okay guy."

Out of the corner of his eye, Joe spotted Frank and Nancy approaching. "Hmm. They don't look too happy."

George waved to them, calling out, "You struck out, huh?"

"No," Frank answered. "We got to first, but then got picked off base. Now we have to wait for another turn at bat."

"Years ago Fripp and Whiteshirt went prospecting for oil on Whiteshirt's land and didn't find any," Nancy explained. "That was when Whiteshirt started thinking about the spirits."

"What does that mean?" Joe asked.

Frank shrugged. "To be continued. What's up with you?"

"I was just telling Joe what Nancy and I talked about with Lieutenant Deerhunter," George said. "We were too busy working to talk earlier." She turned back to Joe. "He showed us this medallion he'd found in Langford's hand. He thought it might have belonged to the killer."

Joe frowned thoughtfully. "What did the medallion look like?"

"Something like this." George began tracing a crude likeness of it in the sand, trying to remember the jagged figures.

Joe's eyes widened. "I've seen that," he said. "Or one just like it."

"Where?" Nancy asked urgently.

Sadness and shock darkened Joe's face. "At Sky's house!"

Chapter

Ten

NANCY SAT BOLT UPRIGHT. "Are you sure, Joe?" she asked.

"She had a necklace," Joe said, "on a display table. It was kind of like a charm bracelet, with lots of these coins dangling from it. I held it in my hands."

"And they were the exact same design?" Frank prodded.

"I'm not an expert," Joe replied. "But they looked the same to me."

"Well," Nancy said, "I guess we're going to Whiteshirt's cabin this afternoon."

Joe stared dejectedly out at the lake. "I'll go

with you, I guess," he said. He picked up a stone and skimmed it on the water.

"Cheer up," Frank said. "She might be innocent. Maybe you two will still go riding off into the sunset together."

Joe smiled. "You never give up, do you?"

"Guys," George spoke up. "I'm going to stick around here, if you don't mind."

"But Ottman gave us the rest of the day off," Joe said. "Wasn't what's-his-name—that guy you were talking to—taking over the site this afternoon for a research project?"

"Jim Haber," George corrected him. "And, yes, he is. It sounded pretty interesting, too. I'd sort of like to see what he's doing."

"Mm-hm," Joe said. "In the interests of archaeology, of course."

George shot him an icy glare. "Just like your visit with Sky was in the interests of investigation, right?"

"Come on," Nancy said with an exasperated sigh. "You coming with us, Frank?"

"No," Frank replied. "I want to call the Network and do a background check on Captain Lorimor. Maybe it's just that he rubbed me the wrong way, but I got the impression he may be hiding something."

"Okay," Nancy said. "Let's meet for dinner around six."

As she and Joe walked to the car, George headed back to the dig.

Frank went to his hotel room and put in a call to a secret toll-free number.

"Vista Real Estate," came an official-sounding voice. It was a code name, and it changed daily.

"Oh, oh, oh, that Shakespearean rag," Frank said.

"I beg your pardon, sir?" the voice responded.

"It's so elegant, so intelligent," Frank answered.

"With whom would you like to speak?"

"Shanti, shanti, shanti." Frank hoped he got the code words right. He had no idea what they meant, and last time he'd been cut off when he had said one wrong word.

There was a series of electronic beeps. Frank felt relieved. He punched in his seven-digit I.D. number and a voice answered, "Yeah, Hardy?"

"Hi, Lifeline," Frank said, using the man's official nickname. "You know, this new code system sounds really dumb. *And* it's tough to remember."

"That's the idea. How are you coming along?"

"Slowly," Frank replied. "I need a report on a Captain Van Allen Lorimor at the Jackson Air Force Base."

"Lorimor—the name rings a bell. Can you

hang on? With this new coprocessor, we should have your info in a few seconds."

"Sure." Frank could hear hollow clicking sounds as Lifeline's fingers rapped on a keyboard.

"Okay," Lifeline said. "Hey, what do you know? It works. Lorimor, Captain Melvin Van Allen—"

"Melvin?"

"Hmmm. Not much here—at least, nothing negative. The guy's forty-five, known for creative strategical and tactical planning, a whole page full of awards and citations. His breastplate must weigh a ton. Let's see, he's a career man, enlisted at eighteen—"

"Eighteen?" Frank asked.

"That makes twenty-seven years in the air force. Pretty amazing."

"What's more amazing is that after all that time, he never rose higher than captain."

"Interesting," Lifeline said. "You know, that's a good point, Hardy. And yet there's not one blemish on his record—at least not in the prelim file."

"Do you have anything else on him?" Frank pressed.

"I'll have to access his classified dossier. Hang on another minute."

On the way to Whiteshirt's cabin, Joe's car slowly rolled by a development of attached adobe houses. Most of them looked alike, differing only in trim and lawn furniture. Gradually they thinned out and gave way to small single-family structures, with one or two horses or cows grazing in the yards behind them. Joe drove until he spotted Sky's house. "This is the one," he said.

He and Nancy got out and walked across the baked dirt yard. From the next yard over, an old woman in a housedress eyed them with a fleeting but intense scrutiny. She disappeared inside her house as Joe rang Sky's bell.

He waited, then rang again.

"I guess she's out," Nancy said.

"This was dumb," Joe replied, rapping on the door. "We should have called."

Turning to go, Joe gave a routine twist to the doorknob. To his and Nancy's surprise, the door swung open.

Inside the light was on and the electric fan was humming. "Hello?" Joe called, stepping through the door.

"Maybe she can't hear us over the fan," Nancy suggested.

Together they walked through the living room. Joe peered into the kitchen. "Sky?"

Curious but not wanting to be a snoop, Nancy stood in the center of the living room and looked around. Many of the artifacts on the tables and shelves did look like they'd come from the Red Clay People dig, but she couldn't tell for sure. She wished she knew more about archaeology and Indian history.

"Well, if she left everything on in the house, I guess she hasn't gone too far," Joe said. "Maybe we should wait."

"Yeah," Nancy replied, "but outside, so the woman next door doesn't call the police."

But as she turned to the door, Joe said, "Hold it a minute!"

"Joe," Nancy said, "this isn't the smartest place to be right now."

Joe was staring intently at one of the tables in the living room. "The necklace isn't there," he said, almost under his breath.

"What?"

"The necklace that had the gold medallions like the one George drew at the lake. It was on that table yesterday, and now it's gone."

Nancy walked slowly back to the center of the room. "Are you sure?"

"I picked it up," Joe said.

"Maybe it fell." Nancy went over to the table and checked behind it. There was nothing but a few dustballs. She and Joe did a quick search of the surrounding floor, with no luck.

As Nancy stood up, she caught a glimpse in through a half-open door beyond the kitchen. Her eyes widened. "Joe?" she gasped. "Look in that bedroom. Do you see what I see?"

Joe stood next to her and saw an enormous wolfskin hanging from the wall inside the room. From the tip of its snout to the claws of its dangling hind legs, it must have been six feet long.

"Well, what do you know?" Joe said softly. "I think we've found our werewolf!"

Chapter

Eleven

WHACK!

The slam of the front door made Nancy and Joe lurch around.

Standing just inside, her eyes blazing with rage, was Sky. "What are you doing in here?" she demanded.

"Sky," Joe said. "The door was open. We thought you were in—"

"And that gave you the right to walk right in and make yourself at home?" She glared at Joe. "My grandfather always told me, 'Once you let a stranger in your house, you can never leave your door unlocked again.' He was right!"

"It wasn't that at all—" Joe tried to say.

"Now I know why you wanted to come in here so badly yesterday," Sky said. "It was a scouting expedition, so you and your girlfriend could rob me!" She stalked across the room toward the phone. "I'm calling the police."

"I wouldn't do that if I were you," Nancy said in a firm voice. "And you know why."

Sky paused. Her hand lingered on the receiver for a few seconds, then fell away. "What are you talking about?" she asked, facing Nancy. Her eyes were still accusing them, but Nancy detected a vulnerability that hadn't been there before.

"You might have to explain your involvement in Dr. Langford's murder," Nancy replied. "And the thefts and the vandalism."

Sky was stunned. She glanced from Nancy to Joe. "That's—that's absurd! How dare you!"

"'Leave the dead alone, or join them,'" Nancy said. "That was the unsigned message left on Langford's desk, made from cut-out letters—almost exactly the warning you gave him in person. There's a necklace that used to be in your living room, and now it's gone. A necklace that has gold coins just like the one found in the hand of Langford's corpse. And the wolfskin that you used to sneak onto the site the next night is hanging on the wall in your bedroom!"

Sky hung her head. "No," she said softly.

Nancy pressed on. "You and your grandfather lost your case in court, so you felt you had to take matters into your own hands."

"Nancy, come on—" Joe murmured. "Ease up."

"Whose side are you on, anyway?" Sky said to Joe with a bitter chuckle. She sank into her sofa and sighed. For a moment her eyes took on a faraway look. "Sit," she said. "If I have to bare my soul, I want us all to be on the same level."

Nancy and Joe quickly sat in armchairs.

"Okay," Sky said. "I did fill in two graves the other night. I started to fill in a third one— the one that collapsed the day after Langford's death—but I heard someone approaching, so I ran away. My digging must have weakened the side, and it fell on Langford later in a delayed reaction or something."

Nancy remembered shovel marks outside the trenches. Sky's explanation made sense.

"I wanted to scare them, make them take us seriously. And I wanted"—her eyes began to well up—"I wanted to preserve my grandfather's dignity. He's obsessed with the evil spirits. They've taken over his mind. People were beginning to laugh at him. He talked about them in court, right in front of the TV cameras. Of course those were the moments they aired on the local news reports."

"So you thought that by sabotaging the dig at night, people might think he wasn't so crazy after all," Nancy said.

Sky nodded sadly. "That was the idea. Then I heard about that volunteer who was hurt. I was so horrified, because that was truly my fault. But Dr. Langford's death?" She heaved a deep sigh. "I was saddened by that, more than you know. Yes, I warned him, but only in person. I would never stoop to sending an anonymous death threat! If he had listened to me, he might still be alive. You say he was murdered, but you don't know if the murderer was flesh and blood, do you? There are many unexplainable things in the gravesites—that's why they should not be entered."

"So of course you've never gone in one of them," Nancy said.

"Of course," Sky repeated solemnly.

"Then where did you get that Red Clay People necklace, and how do you explain the medallion that got into—"

Sky cut Nancy off. "First of all, that necklace wasn't stolen from the site. It's been around our house as long as I can remember. There is no possible way a medallion from it got into Dr. Langford's hands. I'm sure if you look at it you'll see it's complete."

"Then where is it?" Joe interjected.

Sky shrugged. "I don't know. Maybe my

grandfather has it. There's no law that says it has to stay here."

Nancy was beginning to feel bad for Sky. She seemed to be telling the truth. But there were still loose ends.

"What about the wolf skin?" Nancy said.

At that, Sky grew quiet. Frowning, she looked at the floor. "It's—it's Comanche Wolf Medicine. Grandfather keeps it hung there to—to keep the house in harmony among the spirits." She flashed a defiant glance up at Joe and Nancy. "The spirits that killed Dr. Langford."

"What?" Joe said.

Sky's face flushed with renewed anger. "I don't know why I'm telling you this. It's none of your business. You wouldn't understand our customs, anyway."

"Sky," Nancy said as gently as she could, "is all this about trying to protect your grandfather? Was he the one dressed in the pelt last night? Was he out the night Langford was killed? Were *you* there for any reason?"

Sky got up from the sofa and turned her back to Nancy and Joe. Thrusting her hands in her jeans pockets, she walked to the opposite end of the room. "My—my grandfather hasn't been himself lately," she said softly. "The years are wearing him down. The pressures of the court case. He's been disappearing a lot lately, not explaining where he's going . . ."

Sky's voice trailed off. She stood there, with her back still to Nancy and Joe, leaning on a bookcase. They sat patiently, expectantly, not wanting to disturb her.

Suddenly she whirled around. Her face was taut with emotion. "On the night of the murder, my grandfather was very agitated. It wasn't like him—he's usually so calm. He wouldn't tell me why, only that he needed to exorcise the evil from the land, once and for all. When the moon rose that night, he said, he would begin the ritual of the Wolf Medicine.

"I came back early from work and secretly kept an eye on him. He left the house, wearing the wolf pelt. I tried to follow him, but he lost me. I don't know where he went—I don't know what he did." Sky was silently pleading with the other two. "But I swear to you, my grandfather is not a murderer! He is a man of peace. To kill someone by stealth, in cold blood—he could never do it."

Joe's expression said exactly what was on Nancy's mind.

Whiteshirt may be a man of peace, but right now he's a murder suspect.

Chapter

Twelve

Nancy's chicken-fried steak was getting cold that evening as a northern breeze washed over the resort's outdoor dining area. As she described the meeting with Sky, Frank and George listened attentively across the table.

"The thing is," Nancy said, "she insists Whiteshirt isn't *capable* of murder."

"But if his mind is slipping," Frank replied, absently twirling pasta with his fork, "he might be doing things she would never expect."

"I don't know," George said. "It's a long way from Wolf Medicine to murder."

Joe nodded. "That's what I think. Sure,

Whiteshirt was the werewolf, but so what? That doesn't mean he did anything. He might have gone every night to the site and danced around the graves a few times, hummed a few bars, and gone home again."

"Still," Nancy said, "the missing necklace bothers me."

"Maybe, for some reason, he had the necklace with him the night Langford was killed," George speculated. "When Dr. Langford was wandering around the site that night, he might have seen Whiteshirt and thought he was a robber. They got into a fight, Langford grabbed the necklace and ripped off a medallion as Whiteshirt accidentally pushed him into Vault Thirteen.

"You sure you're not a detective?" Joe asked her.

"Yes," George said, beaming. "But it doesn't mean I'm not as smart as one."

Nancy shook her head, her reddish blond hair swirling around her shoulders. "It's a good thought, George, but it doesn't explain the blow to the head Langford got."

Frank checked his watch. "I forgot to tell you—I ran into Saul a few minutes ago, and he says Dr. Ottman is giving a slide show after dinner. It's about Mayan architecture or something. Saul says it's really mandatory for all you volunteers."

"Snooze time," Joe remarked.

"Oh, come on, Joe, I know you wouldn't miss it for the world! Please say you'll sit with me," George said, teasing him.

"What did you find out about Lorimor from the Network?" Nancy asked Frank.

"I made them dig deep for info," Frank said. "Lorimor seemed like a model soldier at first—a long career in the service, awards galore. It seemed strange to me that he never rose higher than captain. Anyway, it turns out that he was involved in a botched secret rescue attempt of American hostages in the Middle East about ten years ago."

"I remember my dad talking about that," Nancy said. "The mission was supposed to be aborted before it started, but a couple of helicopters went ahead anyway and were shot down—"

"And the hostages were kept another two years," Frank continued. "Yep, that's the one. And *Lorimor,* our pal, was the officer in charge who ordered the renegade helicopters to disobey."

"Why wasn't he court-martialed?" Joe asked.

"Apparently Lorimor was very charismatic," Frank said. "Before the incident, he was a rising star and could do no wrong. He knew it, too, and really played the patriot-hero role to the hilt. Apparently he delivered a big, emotional speech about how soft the military had become and claimed that when he was told to retreat, he just snapped. He couldn't turn his back on innocent American citizens. I guess he convinced the tribunal to be lenient, or else he had some high-up support on his side. Whatever it was, he managed to save his hide. But it wasn't without a price. His reputation was tarnished, and promotions just didn't happen for him."

Frank paused and took a sip of water. "Anyway, in recent years Lorimor's been speaking out about the need for trillions and trillions of extra dollars in military spending, nuclear research, the building of shelters, and stockpiling of goods. The Network found some declassified documents that show the military is starting to get embarrassed by him. I think they stuck him out here in the middle of nowhere to teach him a lesson."

"Sounds like a real fanatic," Nancy said.

"He also sounds like somebody who could have his own private plan for saving the country," Joe added. His blue eyes were deadly serious. "Something that might involve hijacking those two missing trucks he supposedly checked through."

"What could he have done with two huge trucks, without somebody seeing?" George asked.

Joe shrugged. "It's a big base. He could have bribed the drivers and figured out a way to hide them on the base. I don't think too many people there question what he does."

"I don't know," Nancy said. "It seems a little farfetched."

"I asked the Network to send us some official papers so we can get into the base and snoop around," Frank continued. "They said we could have them Wednesday morning, the day after tomorrow. They were nervous about sending them to the resort, so they're going to express them to a private carrier company's office in Altus."

"Hey, guys," Nancy said, "we're the last ones here. I think we'd better get to the lecture room."

They cleared their trays and walked quickly to the other wing of the hotel. On the way Nancy and George paired off, walking in front of the Hardy brothers. Nancy gave George a mischievous sidelong smile. "How was your— archaeological discussion with Jim?" she asked.

"Really interesting," George said and grinned tolerantly. "I mean it, Nancy. He's a great guy, and he knows so much! You know, he was really the one who found the site."

Nancy nodded. "That's what Heather said. I thought it was just a rumor."

"Nope. Jim's research showed that the Spanish explorer Coronado had come through here in the 1500s, looking for some mythical

Seven Cities of Gold. Coronado never found the cities, but Jim did some poking around to see why Coronado might have been looking *here,* specifically. He turned up some local legends that suggested to him that the Red Clay People might have lived around here way back when."

"Makes sense," Nancy commented.

"Mm-hm." George nodded, her eyes glowing as she went on with her story. "Anyway, Jim came out to Lake Altus to scout around. He saw a slight depression in the ground where it looked like there had once been a hole. He told his hunch to Langford, and the rest is history! Except," she added hurriedly, "the first place they tried digging didn't pan out. But when they moved about a hundred yards west of that, they found all those gravesites."

George sighed ecstatically. "Oh, Nancy, I could have listened to Jim talk all day! He has a way of making all this dry stuff sound fascinating. He told me all this dirt about Dr. Langford and Dr. Ottman, too."

"Dirt?" Nancy arched a slim eyebrow.

George cringed. "Sorry, no pun intended. I don't know if you noticed, but Dr. Langford was a full professor and Dr. Ottman is still an associate professor—even though Dr. Ottman is one of the country's top Mayan experts."

"No, I hadn't noticed," Nancy said. Ahead of them she saw a few stragglers rushing through the door of one of the conference rooms.

"Well, it's kind of a weird story, and it has to do with the Mayan dig we're going to learn about at this slide show. Dr. Ottman was the one who found the site and asked Dr. Langford to head the dig with him. But after a week or so Dr. Ottman came down with food poisoning and had to go to the hospital, just days before Dr. Langford found an unbelievable collection of artifacts. The artifacts made a huge splash in the archaeological world and earned Dr. Langford his reputation and his professorship!"

"On Dr. Ottman's back," Nancy said. "You know, the more I hear about my dad's old friend, the less I like him."

"Well, Jim says Dr. Ottman got over it," George said. "After all, they were working together on the Red Clay People dig."

Nancy wondered if Dr. Ottman had really gotten over it. Had resentment built up between the two men? Enough to turn Dr. Ottman into a murderer?

For that matter, her suspicions about Jim had flared up again. He had the same motive as Dr. Ottman. Yes, he said he and Dr. Langford had been close, and he didn't seem to mind that the professor had taken credit for his discovery, but that could all be an act.

They went into the conference room. Dozens of folding chairs had been set up in a semicircle facing a large white screen. In the back, Dr. Ottman was standing next to a large, humming slide projector. Nancy, George, Frank, and Joe took four empty seats in the back, just as the lights went out.

The room went pitch-black, then suddenly came to life with a flash of light. A large, half-crumbled ancient building filled the screen.

In a low-pitched monotone, Dr. Ottman announced, "The slides I'm showing were taken at the famous Mayan expedition Dr. Langford and I coheaded about fifteen years ago. Tonight we will see evidence of how themes, methods, and symbols of that culture's art and architecture resurfaced in both the Spiro and the Red Clay People tribes."

Dr. Ottman began to flash dozens of slides, describing each. Nancy's attention slipped until she saw a close-up of an inlaid design on a temple wall. The jagged symbols were familiar.

She leaned over to George and whispered, "That looks like the design on the medallion Deerhunter showed us."

George nodded. "That's not surprising—it's the point of the lecture," she said. "The Spiro and Red Clay People assimilated a lot of Mayan culture."

"Excuse me," Dr. Ottman called out. "Can we keep it quiet so others can hear?"

Nancy and George suppressed guilty giggles. Sighing as she shifted on the uncomfortable folding chair, Nancy resigned herself to sitting out the rest of the show.

That night George was the first to turn off her bedside lamp. "I'm beat, Nancy," she said.

"Me, too," Nancy said. "Listening to Dr. Ottman was like taking a sleeping pill."

"Yeah. Not to mention the sun, and the fact that I lost a few years off my life this morning." She shook her head. "I can't stop thinking of what Deerhunter did. That was pretty mean, making me think he was going to accuse me of murder."

"I know. Not exactly a sensitive technique." Nancy reached over to turn off her own lamp. "He's a strange guy—I can't really figure him out. Anyway, I bet you'll feel better in the morning. Good night."

She heard a rustling and something like *"Mmph lach,"* and she knew George was already out.

But now the episode with Deerhunter was sticking in her mind. What would they tell him the next day? How long would it be before he blew their cover? She remembered his tone of voice, the unreadable way he stared at her when she was trying to decide what to say to him. . . .

As she drifted into sleep, brief images from the day passed through her mind. Loose ends, things she had put off thinking through—a stray statement, a suspicious facial expression, a curious object . . .

Suddenly she sat up in bed. One of the images had stuck—something she had seen in the tent when she was avoiding Deerhunter's stare. A small, familiar-looking box with dials and gauges on it. She had been concentrating so intently she hadn't really focused on it. Now she knew exactly what it was.

"George!" She touched George's shoulder. "I have to tell you something."

"Nnngaaogh," George muttered, slowly rolling around. "What is it?"

"There was a Geiger counter in Dr. Langford's tent," Nancy said urgently.

"Whaaaa?" George squinted sleepily at her.

"It was under his table," Nancy insisted. "I'm sure of it!"

George sat up. "I don't get it, Nan. So what?"

"Why do you think Dr. Langford would have a Geiger counter?"

"I don't know. Maybe some of the stuff in the gravesites is radioactive—" George suddenly fell silent. "Wait a minute."

"Uranium is radioactive, George. Maybe

Dr. Langford had discovered some of it on the site!"

George's excited gasp pierced the silence. "Yeah, some of it that was supposed to be in those shipments Frank and Joe are looking for!"

"Exactly," Nancy said. "Maybe Dr. Langford knew about that stuff—and that's why he was killed!"

Chapter

Thirteen

S o MAYBE THE HARDYS aren't here on a different case after all," George said.

Nancy's mind was racing. "I don't want to jump to conclusions. Maybe Geiger counters are standard tools for archaeologists."

"We can find out," George said. "All we have to do is ask Jim."

"You think he's still awake?" Nancy asked.

"Maybe. It's only ten-thirty."

Nancy flicked on her lamp and hopped out of bed. "I'll be right back."

George threw her covers aside. "I'll come with you."

"I thought you were too tired," Nancy said, pulling her jeans out of the closet.

"Not for this."

Nancy laughed. "I'm sure your interest is strictly archaeological."

"Funny, Nancy. Very funny."

They threw on their clothes and ran outside to get to the other wing. There they climbed to the third floor and knocked on Jim's door.

There was no answer. They tried twice more, then turned away. "Maybe he went out for a night on the town in Altus," Nancy suggested.

"I doubt it," George said. "Knowing him, he's probably over at the site, examining some potsherds."

"Let's go there," Nancy said decisively.

They went back downstairs and headed for a shortcut through a ring of trees that circled the hotel grounds. Beyond the trees was a Dumpster, and just behind that was a small, footworn path that led to the tent.

As they walked around the Dumpster, a distant voice pierced the night silence:

"I will—never again—"

George stopped and listened. "That's Jim," she said.

"Great." They went back around the Dumpster and began to walk toward the sound of the voice. Through the tangle of narrow tree trunks, they could see some movement.

"I know, I know—that's what you told me before—"

That was another familiar voice, one that made Nancy and George stop in their tracks.

"Sky?" Nancy said under her breath.

The two voices jumbled together in what sounded like an argument. Nancy and George stood where they were, not wanting to intrude.

The conversation got louder and more heated, then eased off and stopped. Nancy and George exchanged an uncertain look. When they turned back, they could see Jim and Sky moving from their spot in the trees, heading away from the resort.

"Come on," Nancy whispered.

They walked toward the clearing beyond the trees and caught their first full glimpse of Jim and Sky.

An involuntary gasp caught in George's throat. They were arm in arm, walking slowly and gazing up at the soft amber moon. When Jim turned toward Sky, she stopped walking and wrapped both arms around him. Slowly their lips came together in a long, passionate kiss.

Nancy felt her stomach sink. Despite the orange glow the moonlight cast over the area, George's face was a pale, ghostly white.

The next morning when Nancy awoke, George was already getting dressed. She seemed to be moving a little slower than normal, her expression thoughtful and serious.

"Are you okay?" Nancy asked.

George turned with a start. "Oh! I didn't know you were awake. Yeah, I'm fine." She smiled. "I've been thinking a lot about last night. To tell you the truth, it doesn't bother me as much as I thought it would."

Nancy sat up and stretched. "That's great, George."

"I meant what I said about him yesterday. He's a nice guy, and really smart. But when we were talking, I started looking at him differently. He's so into his work, almost like an excited kid—which is great, but afterward I felt more, well, friendship toward him than—you know—"

"A crush," Nancy said.

"Whatever. Actually, I think it's good that he and Sky are seeing each other. A little sneaky, but good."

"It just makes me wonder, though," Nancy said. "Why *are* they being sneaky? Maybe they're involved in this mess together."

"Maybe," George said with a shrug. "I don't know. I still can't see Jim being involved in anything criminal, especially anything that might harm the science of archaeology. But I guess it wouldn't be such a great idea to ask Jim about that Geiger counter."

Nancy nodded. "It looks like we're finally

going to have to tell Dr. Ottman who we really are. Maybe we should do it before he goes out to the site today."

George made a face. "Do we have to?"

"Well, it's going to be a real hassle making excuses every time we want to leave the site. And besides, he did take over for Dr. Langford." Nancy swung her long legs out of bed and stood up. "Technically, he's the guy we report to."

"What if he decides to send us home?"

Nancy shrugged. "We take that risk. There's no reason for us to be here unless someone wants us."

"Are you kidding? I'm dying to find out what happened! Besides, we can't let Frank and Joe down."

"Don't worry," Nancy said with a smile. "We can always decide to stay here on vacation."

Nancy quickly showered and pulled on a cotton tank top and shorts. Then the two girls went straight to Dr. Ottman's room. He answered their knock with a gruff, "Come in."

He was looking in a closet-door mirror when they went in. Patiently he patted down a few long, dark strands of hair over the bald spot that took up most of his head. Then he turned around. "Yes? What can I do for you?"

"Sorry to bother you, Dr. Ottman," Nancy

said, "but we need a few minutes of your time."

"It's no bother at all," Dr. Ottman said, taking a watch from a huge, messy pile of objects on his dresser.

Nancy carefully explained who she and George were and described their agreement with Dr. Langford. She also said Frank and Joe were involved, not mentioning the details of their own case. Dr. Ottman listened, his heavy brow casting a shadow over his eyes. One by one, he grabbed six rings off his dresser, placing them on his fingers. His solemn, rhythmic "Mm-hm—mm-hm—mm-hm—" punctuated Nancy's talk.

When she finished, he nodded for a few moments and said, "I thought something was up with you two."

A tense silence hung in the air as he plunged his hand once again into the chaos of his dresser top. He picked up the long leather string that he wore around his neck every day. The magnifying glass, keys, and Swiss army knife jangled as they left the dresser. "You know," he finally said, "You have just allayed one of my greatest fears."

"I beg your pardon?" Nancy replied.

Dr. Ottman smiled for the first time since they'd been there. "I was dreading the idea of having to trust this whole thing to Lieutenant Deerhunter."

Nancy blinked in surprise. George let out a little laugh.

"The thing is, Dr. Ottman," Nancy continued, "we're not going to be the greatest volunteers. We'll have to leave unexpectedly, bother people with questions——"

"Fine," Dr. Ottman said with a wave of his hand. "It'll be worth it if you can help solve this thing. Besides, if anything, I have too many volunteers."

Nancy immediately felt her entire body relax. Maybe now, finally, Dr. Ottman wouldn't seem like such an ogre. "By the way," she said, "are Geiger counters used on archaeological sites like this?"

Dr. Ottman looked at her curiously. "No. Why?"

"There's one under Dr. Langford's table in the tent," Nancy replied.

"Really?" Dr. Ottman said. "Are you sure?"

"I think so," Nancy said.

Dr. Ottman raised his eyebrows. "Strange. Let's take a look."

They all walked over to the tent. Dr. Ottman held the flap aside as the girls entered the tent. Nancy ducked under the table, pulled out the small metallic box, and gave it to Dr. Ottman.

He examined it. "What do you know? It is a Geiger counter, all right. Maybe Tod thought there was nuclear waste on the land." He shuddered. "That's all we need, isn't it?"

Putting the box down on the table, he said, "Now, if you'll excuse me, I've got to get back and have some breakfast before I begin my day. Hope to see you at work."

They left the tent. Dr. Ottman headed to the resort, and Nancy and George went over the ridge to the dig. As they topped the rise they spotted Frank and Joe hard at work in one of the trenches.

"We came over here looking for you, and instead we got drafted into hard labor," Joe complained. He ran a dirt-caked hand through his blond hair, then remembered the dirt. He snorted in disgust.

"Relax," George said. "You guys may have the shortest archaeological careers in history. Nancy told Dr. Ottman about us and he's not going to be breathing down our necks."

Joe dropped his sifter. "Great. Let's go water-skiing."

"Not so fast," Nancy said. "There's a new twist. There's a Geiger counter in Dr. Langford's tent, and Dr. Ottman says that's not usual equipment for archaeologists."

"Whoa!" Joe said. "Looks like we may be in the right place, after all."

"If Langford knew something about radioactivity on this land," Frank said, "and somebody knew he knew—"

"We may have our motive for the killing,"

Nancy finished for him. Right in sync, as usual!

"And if nuclear stuff has been hidden here," Joe said, "Whiteshirt probably knows about it, since he owns the land."

"I think we should try Fripp again," Frank suggested. "Get him to open up about Whiteshirt."

"I'm with you," Joe said.

"Hold it," Nancy warned. "One of us should stay here in case anything comes up."

The three of them looked at George. She laughed. "I guess I'm elected."

"Thanks, George," Nancy said. "We'll see you back here in a few hours."

Soon they were speeding along the highway. The shimmering heat that rose from the asphalt made the town of Altus appear to be a desert mirage. As they drew nearer, though, the buildings became solid.

"High-class place," Joe said as Frank parked in front of the dilapidated Altus Professional Building.

"At least it's easier to stop by unannounced," Frank replied.

Inside the building, the clattering of typewriters mixed with a chorus of one-sided phone conversations and the rhythmic whir of a copy machine. The reception desk was empty, so they walked straight to the back.

As they passed the broom closet, they could

hear muffled voices coming from Fripp's office at the end of the hall. Joe walked up to the closed wooden door and drew his hand back to knock.

"You leave Whiteshirt to me!"

The words were clear as day. It was Fripp's voice, and it was accompanied by a pounding noise.

Joe pulled his arm back. There was a sharp *tap, tap, tap* of footsteps on Fripp's linoleum-tiled floor.

The three of them eyed one another. Out of the corner of her eye, Nancy spotted the half-open broom closet door. "Come on!" she whispered.

She scampered inside, followed by Frank and then Joe. As Joe pulled the door behind him, leaving it open a crack, they could hear the click of Fripp's doorknob being pushed open.

Nancy held her breath. She was backed up tight against a damp cold-water pipe. In the near-darkness she could make out Joe pressed to the door's crack as a person passed through the hallway.

Slowly Joe shut the closet door. The room was now completely dark except for a thin rectangle of light tracing the doorframe.

"Did you see him?" Frank whispered.

"Yes," Joe said, his voice charged with excitement. "It was Captain Lorimor!"

Chapter
Fourteen

ORIMOR! WHAT DOES *he* have to do with this?" Nancy asked.

"Whatever it is, Whiteshirt's involved, too," Joe answered. "They were talking about him."

"This is unbelievable," Frank said under his breath. "Half of Oklahoma is involved in this case!"

"I don't think we should see Fripp until we've thought this through," Nancy said. "Can we go someplace to talk? My back is getting wet from this stupid pipe."

Joe silently turned the doorknob, eased the door open a crack, and peeked through. "Come on," he whispered over his shoulder.

The three of them slipped into the hallway. As they scurried toward the front of the building, Nancy thought she heard a click behind them. She spun around, but saw only closed doors on both sides of the hallway.

They ran outside and jumped into the car. Joe stepped on the gas and drove off in a hurry.

As they rounded a corner onto a main street, Joe said, "Let's figure this out. Fripp's trying to stop the digging on Whiteshirt's land. Fripp was just arguing with Lorimor. Their argument had something to do with Whiteshirt. What do those three have in common?"

Frank answered. "If Lorimor took that nuclear material, as we think he might have, he'd need a place to store it, right? Well, put yourself in Lorimor's shoes. Just outside the air force base there's this large, virtually unused tract of land. An old Indian guy owns it, and he's desperate for money. If you're Lorimor, and you find out about this land, what do you do?"

"You contact the old man—or maybe his lawyer—and arrange to bury the nuclear junk on the land," Nancy said, "paying everybody a nice big fee."

"Then this university comes along and decides to start digging on the land," Joe interjected. "The guy in charge has a Geiger counter, and stumbles on the radioactive stuff—maybe starts digging it up. So you kill him off."

"Hold it," Nancy said. "Dr. Langford started this dig about six weeks ago. When were the shipments lost?"

"Two months ago," Joe replied. "It fits perfectly!"

"No, too many loose ends," Nancy said, shaking her head. "First of all, with all his beliefs about evil spirits, I don't think Whiteshirt would allow radioactive material to be buried on his land. And even if he did—even if all this Wolf Medicine stuff is an act—why would Whiteshirt and Fripp lease the land to the university if they knew what was hidden on it, let alone allow digging?"

"Any number of reasons," Frank answered. "The land had hundreds of acres. It couldn't have seemed likely the university would choose the exact spot where the radioactive material was buried. Or maybe Fripp might have arranged the nuclear burial behind Whiteshirt's back. Then Whiteshirt, not knowing about it, might have struck an agreement with the university's lawyers without consulting Fripp."

"Yes, but if Lorimor buried the stuff in the Red Clay People site, wouldn't he have come across artifacts himself?" Nancy asked.

Frank waved his hand dismissively. "Broken pieces of clay, arrowheads—whoever Lorimor hired to do the burying wouldn't think any of that was special. Even if Lorimor did it himself, he probably wouldn't have cared. This whole area was inhabited by Indians at one time. It takes an expert to know which relics are important."

"Okay," said Nancy, still piecing things together, "then how did Dr. Langford become suspicious enough to get a Geiger counter? You can't just look at something and say, 'Gee, I wonder if that's radioactive,' can you?"

"If it's in containers that say Radioactive, you can," Joe said. "From what I've seen in news reports, that's how the stuff is packaged."

"Then he wouldn't need a Geiger counter!" Nancy shot back. "Dr. Langford could read!"

Everybody was silent. After a long moment Frank said, "If we can figure that one out, we may have this case in the bag. Can you get the Geiger counter, Nancy?"

Nancy nodded. "Sure. It's still in the tent, as far as I know. As long as Lieutenant Deerhunter isn't hanging around, I should have no problem."

"Good," Frank said. "If we get back during the afternoon break, the site'll be empty. We can take the Geiger counter and test for radioactivity. If we find it, maybe we'll figure out what tipped Langford off."

"One thing about this gives me the creeps," Nancy said. "We're assuming Dr. Langford either found radioactivity or was near it. If that's so, why did he let the digging continue? Wasn't he concerned about his volunteers' safety—not to mention his own?"

"Everyone says Langford was a zealous guy," Frank said. "This dig was going to make him famous. Maybe he was covering up what he found."

"I hate to say this, folks," Joe said. "But what about *our* safety? If that place is a nuclear dump, we're rubbing our faces in it."

Frank sighed. "Well, there's always the chance that we're wrong about all of this."

"Yeah," Joe said. "And there's always the chance that we'll go back to Bayport with our hair falling out."

"Gross, Joe," Nancy said. "Cut it out."

It was the last thing anybody said. Gloom settled over them like a stifling blanket as the car sped along the highway to the Quartz Mountain dig site.

Half an hour later, Nancy and George emerged from the headquarters tent, toting Nancy's duffel bag. "The coast is clear," George said.

"Of course it is," Nancy replied. "It must be a hundred and five degrees. We're the only fools not spending our break at the lake."

"Well, if we find what we think we're going to find, we're going to have a better tan than anybody else." George attempted a laugh, but it came out weak and forced.

Frank and Joe were waiting outside Red Clay Vault One. "We might as well start here," Frank said. "It'll be easiest to keep track if we do this in numerical order."

"Are you sure you can work this thing?" George asked.

"I've done it before," Frank said, releasing the microphone-like detector from its attachment on the side of the box.

The four of them climbed into the trench. At the bottom, Frank flicked a switch and put the detector to the ground. A steady *tick-tick-tick* began.

Frank stared at a gauge on the side of the box. "Hmm, it's slightly higher than normal."

"Oh, boy," Joe said. "When do I get to see my bones through my skin?"

"No, no," Frank replied. "Look at this. It's still below the danger zone. The higher reading is abnormal, but it could just mean the machine isn't calibrated right."

They went around the entire floor of the trench, then went to the other ones. They sneaked under the ropes that cordoned off the collapsed trenches and passed the counter over as much area as they could. Throughout, the ticking was more or less the same, right up through the last trench, Red Clay Vault Thirteen.

Taking a brief tour around the edge of the entire site, Frank finally shut the machine off. "All of them are consistently a little above normal," he said. "But no hot spots."

"Want to bet?" George said, wiping her sweaty brow with the back of her arm.

"I mean, no places with huge amounts of radiation," Frank elaborated, "like there would be if we had found the nuclear load."

"Well, it was a nice theory," Nancy said. "Now it's back to the drawing board." She began walking toward the shade of the nearby bluff.

The others trudged behind her. "Hey, come on! I'm glad we were wrong," Joe said. "Aren't you?"

"Sure." Nancy sat down in the shadow that was just beginning to grow under the bluff. "It fit together so well, though. I can't believe we were so far off."

In the dead of the hot afternoon silence, the sound of footsteps above them was unexpectedly loud. Nancy looked up to see Jim and Sky coming down the path over the bluff.

"Hi!" Jim called out. He seemed to be slightly startled. "What are you guys doing here during break?" Before anyone could answer, Jim gave a puzzled frown and added, "Is that a Geiger counter?"

"Uh, yes," Frank answered. "We were asked to do a routine search for, um, naturally occurring radioactive material." He smiled and wiped his brow. "Unfortunately, this is the best time to do it—when the place is empty."

"You're really doing it the hard way," Sky said. "You ought to call this lawyer I know in Altus—Greg Fripp."

"Fripp?" Frank repeated, trying to conceal his surprise.

"Yes," Sky said enthusiastically. "He used to work in the Jackson County geological abstracts office. He could answer your question in a second. He knows everything there is to know about this area. I think I have his card somewhere."

As Sky rummaged through her shoulder bag, Frank glanced sideways at the others. Their weary, sunburned faces all had identical hopeful expressions. It was clear they were all feeling the same way.

Their dying case had just gotten a jump start.

As soon as Jim and Sky had gone, Nancy returned the Geiger counter to the headquarters tent. Then the four of them headed back to the resort to clean up and drive into town.

"For once, I'm glad you're driving. This sedan is a clunker," Joe complained as they sped along the highway. "We really should have rented a Jeep, Frank."

"This car works just fine," his older brother

replied calmly. "You just want a Jeep so you can look cool and impress girls."

Nancy and George burst out laughing. Joe's face turned a little red, but he took it good-naturedly.

They arrived at the Altus Professional Building a little after two-thirty, and the first floor was as bustling as ever. The receptionist spotted them coming in and said, "Mr. Fripp's people, right?"

"Right," Frank said.

The receptionist nodded smugly. "I remember you from yesterday. He's not back from lunch. You want to go back and wait? He should be here any minute."

"Thanks," Frank replied.

He went to Fripp's office, followed by the others. The door was unlocked, so they walked in.

It looked as though an avalanche of paper had fallen into the room. Every flat surface, including two folding chairs, was covered with legal documents.

"Make yourselves at home!" Joe said with mock congeniality.

"Looks like he's got a big case," George commented. "What if he's gone for hours?"

"We might as well make ourselves comfortable," Nancy said. She began lifting a stack of papers off one of the chairs. "We'll just put these directly under the chairs, exactly as they—"

Suddenly she stopped. Her eyes lit on the top page of the stack. Under the word *Declassified,* which was stamped in red letters, a title jumped out at her.

U.S. GOVERNMENT STUDY OF RADIOACTIVE LEAKAGE IN QUARTZ MOUNTAIN NUCLEAR WASTE DISPOSAL SITE

Nancy dropped the stack and snatched up the report. The study had been done fifteen years ago, according to the date on the cover. Flipping past the title page, she began to read furiously.

"What is it, Nancy?" George asked.

"Listen to this!" Nancy said. She read aloud: "'The disposal of various early byproducts of nuclear bomb testing, carried out in a regular, covert, and legal federal program throughout the fifties and sixties, was stopped last year for reasons of concern for public safety. At some sites it is now apparent that low-level amounts of radioactive material have leached into the surrounding soil. It is to be emphasized that the level of radioactivity is well below that considered harmful to human beings. The area most affected is located between approximately 34.7 degrees north to 35 degrees north and 99.3 degrees west to 99.5 degrees west, in the territory west of Lake Altus—'"

Nancy looked up, her eyes wide. "This is incredible. The Red Clay People land is a government nuclear dump!"

Chapter

Fifteen

JOE LET OUT a low whistle of astonishment. "The curves keep coming!" he said.

Frank shook his head. "I don't get it. If the waste started leaching out that long ago, why weren't our readings higher?"

Nancy continued reading. " 'A clean-up program is being organized, to proceed as a top-secret operation and to be carried out under cover of darkness in the worst-afflicted areas.' They must have mopped most of it up back then. But obviously they couldn't get it all."

"Leaving low levels of radiation over the whole area," George said.

"Keeping the Red Clay People toasty warm

in their graves," Joe remarked with a grim smile.

Frank peered out Fripp's door. "I think we got more than we came here for. I also think we should leave and make sure the room looks like it hasn't been entered."

Quickly Nancy replaced the pile on the chair. The four of them left the office and walked back up the hallway. As they passed the receptionist, George said, "The door was locked. We'll try again later."

"Can I take your names—" the woman began. Before she could finish the sentence, they were out the door.

"I'm starving," Joe said as soon as they were on the sidewalk. "I vote a time-out for lunch before we start tackling this thing again."

"You got it," Frank said. They all piled into the car, and Frank drove down the street to a fast-food restaurant with a drive-through window. As they sat in the parking lot, munching on burgers and fries, they talked about the case.

"This could explain a lot of things," Frank said, squeezing ketchup on his double cheeseburger. "Like why Whiteshirt wasn't able to farm the land. The radiation is low for humans, but probably not for vegetation."

"No wonder Whiteshirt thought his land had evil spirits on it," Nancy said from the front seat next to Frank.

"He was right," Joe added. "The evil spirits were the ghosts of a nuclear bomb!"

George swallowed a sip of chocolate shake. "This also explains Dr. Langford's death," she added excitedly. "The government killed him off because he found out about the dump and was going to expose the whole thing!"

"Bzzzzt! Sorry, wrong answer!" Joe said, in an imitation of a TV game show. "The report says declassified, which means anybody could have access to it. The government can't be too worried about leakage."

"Leakage! Oops, Freudian slip," Nancy interjected with a laugh. She tilted her cup to get the last drops of her orange soda.

"Fripp probably picked the report up through his connections with the geological abstracts office," Frank said. "The question is, what does he want to do with it?"

"Use it to strengthen his case against the dig?" George said. "On the grounds that it might be harmful to the volunteers?"

"That makes sense," Nancy said. "But now there are a whole bunch of loose ends again— like why Dr. Langford had the Geiger counter and why he was killed."

Frank exhaled. "And we still don't know what Lorimor has to do with this, let alone what happened to the two trucks and their contents!" He wolfed down the last of his burger, crumpled up the wrapper, and put it into the cardboard container. "I'm going to start driving. Hang on to your food."

He pulled out of the parking lot. Before long, he was driving up the entrance ramp to the expressway.

Nancy stared out the window, deep in thought. "It's sad," she said. "All this horrible stuff destroying the land—and it's just going to sit there until it decays or somebody cleans it up."

"Or steals it," Frank suggested. His face lit up. "Hey! Maybe that's the key!"

"Why would anyone steal something like that?" George asked.

"Nuclear waste is valuable stuff in the terrorist black market," Frank replied. "It can be used in making new weapons. If some unscrupulous organization heard about the stash in the dig site, they just might kill to get—*hey!*"

To their left, a dark blue pickup with tinted windows edged dangerously close. With a sickening crunch, it pressed against the side of the car.

Frank leaned on the horn. "What are you doing, you stupid—"

"Frank!" came a frantic warning from Joe. "Watch out!"

As the car careened onto the grassy shoulder, Nancy couldn't hold in her scream of fright. The car was heading straight for a concrete bridge abutment!

Chapter

Sixteen

Y EEEEEAAAAHHH!" The cry flew out of Joe's mouth.

Nancy braced herself. She could feel the constraints of her shoulder belt, but it wasn't too comforting.

The car jounced violently over ruts, and as the bridge raced toward them, Nancy closed her eyes.

Suddenly her body slammed against the right-side door. She felt herself sinking, as if the car were about to tip over. Her eyes popped open.

"Hang on!" Frank shouted through clenched teeth. His knuckles were white, gripping the steering wheel, yanking it all the way to the right.

The car swerved, digging a deep rut in the soil. It angled away from the bridge. Metal screeched as the left bumper made contact.

But Frank had already managed to steer the car almost parallel to the bridge. The bumper bounced off, deflecting the car. It slowed down and rolled to a stop, its left side inches from the abutment.

No one spoke. The *whirr, whirr* of bridge traffic continued as if nothing had happened.

"Well!" Joe said, exhaling a whoosh of air. "What were we saying? Something about fanatics who kill over nuclear waste? Hey, good driving, big brother!"

"Frank, you're amazing," Nancy said, her voice shaky. "I didn't think we'd make it."

"Uh-huh," Frank answered, his hands still tight around the steering wheel. "I didn't, either."

"Are you all right?" George asked.

"Sure, sure," Frank replied.

"Frank," Joe said gently. "You can let go now."

Frank's hands fell off the wheel. His body slumped back against his seat, and just the trace of a relieved smile flickered across his face.

Suddenly Nancy's jaw dropped open. "Frank!" she shouted, staring at a pool of dark red liquid growing on the breast pocket of his white T-shirt. "Quick, move into the passenger seat!" She lifted herself off the seat, arching her body so Frank could slip underneath.

Frank shot her a confused look. "What? Why—"

"Your chest!" Nancy said. "You've been hurt!"

Frank looked down. For a moment he was too shocked to do anything. Then he dipped a finger in the oozing red mass and brought it to his lips.

"Not bad," he said with a smile. "But I would have preferred it on my french fries."

He reached into his shirt pocket, pulling out a ruptured plastic ketchup container. "Must have been in the wrong place when I hit the steering wheel."

In the backseat George was the first to explode with laughter. Joe joined her, and then Frank. Still arched awkwardly over the passenger seat, Nancy felt suddenly very foolish. She plopped back down, stewed for a moment, then let her own gale of laughter cleanse away the tension.

"Not bad!" Nancy called out as Frank and Joe pulled up to the resort in a new rented sedan the next morning.

Frank leaned out the window. "Joe wanted a Jeep or a sports car. He's sulking."

"No I'm not," Joe said from the passenger seat. "It's fine—for a sensible middle-aged couple with two kids and a dog."

Nancy and George laughed. "What about the damage to the other one?" Nancy asked.

"The insurance on my dad's credit card covered it," Frank said. "But the guy at the rental agency didn't look too happy. He wouldn't let us rent any of the nice cars—that's how we ended up with this baby." He took the car out of Park and put it into Drive. "Anyway, we're off to Altus. If the Network hasn't screwed up, we should be getting our fake clearance papers. Then it's back to Jackson Air Force Base to track down those nuclear shipments."

"There are monster hangars just sitting there empty," Joe said. "That's where I'd hide the stuff if I were Lorimor."

"What did the police have to say about our mysterious 'accident'?" George wanted to know.

Joe frowned darkly. "Not much. Said they'd check into it, but without a license number it would be tough to track down the driver."

"Any ideas about who drove us off the road?" George asked.

Frank shook his head. "Half the people in Oklahoma drive blue pickups."

"What are you guys doing today?" Joe asked.

"Deerhunter called us this morning," Nancy said. "He wants to meet us at the site. Maybe he has a new lead."

"Hope so," Frank said, pulling away. "Meet you back here at break time?"

"Okay," Nancy said.

As the sedan drove away, Nancy and George walked to the dig site. There, Deerhunter was sitting in his Jeep with the air-conditioning on. When he saw them, he climbed out. "'Morning," he said. "You two have any news for me?"

"We sure do," Nancy said. "Whiteshirt may be involved. According to his granddaughter Sky, he's been acting strange lately. He's been leaving his house at night wearing a wolf costume—he did it the night of the murder."

"Comanche Wolf Medicine," Deerhunter interrupted.

"How did you know?" Nancy asked.

"I'm part Comanche myself," Deerhunter said. "My grandfather used to hang a wolf skin in his house. I know Whiteshirt puts his on sometimes. I'm not sure what it signifies."

"The night after the murder—the night George left her wallet in the trench—we saw him, or *somebody,* wearing a wolfskin and poking around by Red Clay Vault Thirteen," Nancy said. "So it follows that he could have gone there in his costume the night Dr. Langford was killed."

147

"So you think the old man killed Langford?" Deerhunter asked skeptically.

"I think it's a possibility," Nancy said. "Joe Hardy saw a charm necklace in Whiteshirt's house that might have had the coin you showed us the other day on it."

Deerhunter kept staring at Nancy, not saying a word. Nancy stared at the two images of herself reflected in his mirrored lenses. "And —that's our news!" she finally said.

George nodded in agreement.

"That's it?" Deerhunter asked.

"Well, yes," Nancy said, beginning to feel nervous. She didn't want to mention anything about the nuclear waste because it might force her to talk about Frank and Joe's case, and it was really up to them to talk to the police about that. But was it possible that Deerhunter knew something about it anyway?

Deerhunter pushed himself away from the Jeep, shaking his head. "I already talked to Whiteshirt. He admits he was out doing the Wolf Medicine chant the night Langford got killed—but not at the gravesite."

He turned his back and reached for the door.

Nancy gritted her teeth. She had a feeling Deerhunter wanted to draw her out, for dramatic effect. She played into it. "Then where was he?"

"In a cave," Deerhunter said over his shoul-

der. He pointed off toward the mountains.
"It's way up on Quartz Mountain, at the edge
of his property."

George spoke up. "How do you know he's
telling the truth?"

At that Deerhunter turned around. He took
off his glasses and gave George a stern look.
"Look, I may not believe in the old-time
rituals, Comanche or otherwise, but I respect
the traditions. If Whiteshirt tells me he was in
a cave, he was in a cave." He opened his car
door and hopped inside. Lowering the tinted
window, he said, "Besides, I went up there the
day the body was found and checked it out.
There are signs—fresh ashes from a fire that
had burned for several hours, things like that.
It's clear that someone was there all night."

With a roar of the engine and a cloud of
dust, Deerhunter took off.

"Thank you for telling us where it is,"
George muttered.

"George, this is getting so weird," Nancy
said, shaking her head. "What was Whiteshirt
up to? Is he really crazy, or is there some
thread of logic in his mind?"

George shrugged. "I guess the only one who
knows the answer to that is Whiteshirt."

"Okay," Nancy said, her brow furrowed.
"I'm Whiteshirt. My land has been destroyed
by nuclear waste, but I don't know that. I'm

convinced there are spirits at work, and they're being released faster by Langford's digging. So I go to the dig site to do an exorcism. But the night before, I went to another place—a cave. Why? Why is the cave so important to me?"

"Maybe you figured out the spirits were stronger there," George suggested.

Nancy's blue eyes began to blaze. "That's it! George, you're a genius!"

"What did I say?"

"We're going to that cave right now."

George stared at Nancy as if she were crazy. "How? Are we going to contact one of the spirits for directions?"

"Nope, we're going to contact Sky." A smile grew across Nancy's face. "But first we're taking a detour to the tent to get the Geiger counter!"

Less than an hour later, with the morning sun behind them, Nancy and George followed Sky up a winding mountain path. Prickly burrs clung to the bottom of Nancy's chinos and made her glad she had decided against shorts that day. The higher they climbed, the more Nancy felt the weight of the Geiger counter, and she switched it from hand to hand.

Before long Nancy became short of breath. Both she and George were huffing and puffing, walking at least twenty yards behind Sky, who seemed to scamper up effortlessly.

"What's with us?" George said between gulps for air. "We sound like—a couple of middle-aged tourists. I thought we were—in pretty good shape."

"We are, but we're not used to climbing in this heat," Nancy replied. "Sky is."

Ahead of them, Sky approached what seemed to be the crest of the hill. She stopped for a long moment, then turned around. "I'm having second thoughts."

George rolled her eyes. "After all this?"

"You say you are detectives," Sky began. "You say you need to solve a crime that involves this cave, but you won't be specific. How do I know you won't disgrace my grandfather?"

"Sky, what we're doing—may save your grandfather," Nancy insisted. She paused, catching her breath. "There's a chance—just a chance—that he may be onto something that will get him in big trouble. Please, we won't disturb anything in the cave. Just let me take a reading."

Sky turned from Nancy to George, as if trying to read the truth in their eyes. Finally she sighed and started back up. "Follow me."

At the very top of the mountain was a long, straight ridge, completely barren. No weeds grew between the cracks in the rocks, no clumps of grass poked out of the ground. Sky walked right up to the edge. Then, just as Nancy expected her to stop, she jumped off.

Nancy felt her heart skip a beat. "Sky!" she and George shouted in unison.

Sky's face popped up over the ridge. "Yes?"

Nancy and George couldn't hold back nervous giggles. "You could have warned us you were going to do that!" George said.

"Oh, sorry." Sky smiled contritely. "I didn't mean to scare you. Come down."

They both peered over the ridge to see a wide, flat ledge of rock. Beyond it was a steep drop to a pile of fallen boulders below. "Comfy," George remarked.

Sky helped them down. Standing on the ledge, Nancy found herself staring into the triangular opening of a dark cave. A sudden blast of wind made a low, moaning sound emanate from within.

George shuddered. "Suddenly I want to be back home in River Heights."

"As you can see," Sky said, "this ridge is the perfect natural camouflage for the cave. From the approach we took, it's impossible to stumble onto it. It has always been a secret, cherished place for my grandfather, and he grieves about the spirits having taken root here."

Nancy reached into her pocket and pulled out a penlight. Shining its slender beam inside the cave, she walked in.

She bounced the light around the walls, judging the boundaries of the cave: about twenty feet deep, fifteen feet across, seven feet high. This would be quick work. She stepped toward the back, with George and Sky behind her, then turned around. "Here," she said, giving the flashlight to George. "Can you shine this on the Geiger counter?"

George held the light steady as Nancy flicked on the machine, exactly as she'd seen Frank do it. Holding the sensor in her right hand, she thrust it toward the back of the cave.

It started ticking before she moved her hand.

No—shrieking was more like it. In the confines of the cave, the chattering sound seemed as loud as a jet taking off. Nancy took back the flashlight and shone it into the recesses of the cave.

When she moved toward the back, the noise got even louder. She brought the sensor closer, pinpointing the area that gave off the most radiation.

The noise was now constant. It sounded like loud static. George covered her ears with her hands, and her expression was pained.

"Turn it off!" Sky demanded.

In response, Nancy flicked off the machine.

The silence that followed made Nancy's ears pop. Her flashlight traced an area along the back of the cave. The floor was smooth, except for an area about six feet square in the back. Nancy took a look at the loose soil, the outline of a large hole.

"Well, folks," she said, her voice a mixture of triumph and grimness, "it looks like we've found our nuclear waste."

Chapter

Seventeen

N ANCY, LET'S GET out of here," George said. It was Nancy's first thought, too. She and George quickly left the cave, followed by Sky.

"What's going on here?" Sky demanded. "Is this what you were looking for this afternoon —the naturally occurring radioactivity?"

"I don't think that level of radiation occurs naturally," Nancy said. She took a deep breath. It was going to be hard to break this news to Sky. "We have reason to believe the government dumped nuclear waste on your grandfather's land years ago. We thought it was over near the Red Clay People site, but I believe it's here now."

Sky looked flabbergasted. "How do you know this?"

"When you told us about Fripp this afternoon—" George began.

"You said he worked in the geological abstracts office," Nancy said, cutting her off. "We found out from them about some declassified information describing the dump." It wasn't the truth, but it wasn't exactly a lie. She didn't want to reveal what they had seen in Fripp's office—not to a client of his who might report it back to him.

"I—I can't believe it," Sky said. "Wouldn't they have asked first? Wouldn't we have seen them do it?"

"It happened many years ago, way before there were any regulations governing nuclear waste disposal," Nancy said.

"I don't know, Nancy." George was shaking her head, looking at the cave. "That hole back there didn't look like it was dug in the fifties."

Nancy frowned. She'd been so excited about the finding, and so concerned about telling Sky, that she hadn't thought about that. "You're right, George. The soil was still loose."

"Maybe they moved it there recently from somewhere else," George suggested.

"Could be," Nancy agreed. "Frank did find some low-level radiation around the dig site. If the waste had been stored there first, then moved to the cave, maybe it left trace amounts."

"That's right!" George said, her voice growing excited. "And remember what Jim said to me? Six weeks ago he discovered the dig site when he saw a place in the ground *where there'd been some digging.* He assumed it had happened ages ago, but maybe the government had done it and carefully covered it up!"

"Not carefully enough," Nancy said.

"Hold it a minute," Sky said. "You're fitting pieces together but not seeing the whole puzzle. If what you say is true, why would the government have moved this material? Did they just look at the land and say, 'Hmm, I think this would go better up in a cave'?"

"That's a good question," Nancy said.

A look of alarm came over George's face. "Nancy, what if this is the stuff that Frank and Joe are looking for?"

"*More* nuclear material?" Sky asked incredulously.

"I don't think so," Nancy answered. "Chances are that anything shipped by truck these days would be stored in sealed, lead-lined containers. Only tiny amounts of radiation would leak out. The geiger counter wouldn't have gone crazy like that. No, my hunch is that it's the waste."

"This is outrageous!" Sky cried. "The university is trashing an entire people's past, and now the government is destroying the present and the future! No wonder this land has been barren and hostile. No wonder my grandfather is being driven crazy. He sensed something was wrong. That's why he was up here chanting!"

George nodded ruefully. "He came to exorcise evil spirits, but little did he know what he was up against."

"The thing is," Nancy said, "*how* did he sense this? How did he know?"

Sky scowled angrily. "Don't underestimate the ways of the Comanche, Nancy Drew."

In the store marked Super-Mail Night and Day—Altus Branch, Frank and Joe waited while a clerk searched through a binful of multicolored boxes and envelopes. "Ah, Hardy," he said. "Here it is. Just came in."

"Thanks," Frank said, taking the small envelope from the man's hand. Frank ripped the envelope open, holding it close to his chest. He pulled out two smaller envelopes. In each of them was a laminated photo ID. Frank picked his up and smiled. The photo showed him, from the chest up, in an air force uniform. Below the picture was the name Nathaniel Rogers. "The superimposition is perfect!" he said softly. "And they even picked a decent name for me."

"Kind of makes me want to enlist," Joe said, admiring his own ID, which said Jonathan Rogers.

"If this doesn't work, I hope the Network can bail us out of the slammer."

Slipping the cards in their wallets, the brothers headed outside and went to the car. "You want to drive?" Frank asked.

"I'll reserve the good cars," Joe said with a smile as he got into the passenger seat. "You can drive the family sedans. After all, you proved yourself in a crisis yesterday."

"Nice guy."

Frank climbed in and steered the car out to the highway. In a little while they were outside the Jackson Air Force Base guardhouse.

"Yes, sir," the guard said.

Frank breathed an inward sigh of relief. It wasn't the same guard; the other guy might have recognized them and asked questions. He and Joe opened their wallets to him.

"Mm-hm," the guard said, taking the wallets and scrutinizing the cards. "From out of state, huh?"

"Yes," Frank said.

The guard squinted at him. "Nat or Nate?"

Frank stared back blankly. He hadn't expected there to be any code words involved. "Excuse me?"

The guard closed up both wallets and

handed them back. "I have a cousin named Nathaniel. My uncle and aunt called him Nat when he was a kid, then he decided he was a Nate."

"Oh!" Frank said, grabbing his wallet. "Just —Nathaniel."

"Johnny!" Joe blurted out, just in case the guard was going to ask him the same question.

Frank stepped on the gas as the guard went back into the guardhouse.

"Ho!" the guard shouted. "I have to give you a parking pass! Which parking lot are you going to?"

Frank stopped and backed up to the guardhouse. "Uh, which one are we going to, Johnny?" he asked Joe.

Caught off-guard, Joe stammered, "Uh— well, the one over to the right."

"We don't know the number of the lot," Frank said, "but it's next to the building where Captain Lorimor works."

"That's Lot Eight," the guard replied, tossing a small laminated pass on Frank's dashboard. "Follow the road around to the right."

"Thanks," Frank said.

He drove through the open gate and into the parking lot. "I don't know how long this is going to work," Frank said. "Lorimor may be looking out for us."

"He won't recognize the car," Joe said.

"And we're on the opposite side of the building from his office, so he won't see us. Even if he calls the guard, he's only seen two guys named Nathaniel and Jonathan Rogers—"

"One blond, the other dark-haired, both in their late teens, one of whom mentioned Lorimor's name. Nah, Lorimor wouldn't be able to tell at all!" Frank finished sarcastically.

"Oh—yeah," Joe said, raising his eyebrows. "I guess we'd better hurry."

Frank pulled quickly into a spot near the parking-lot exit. He and Joe walked around the edge of the lot, taking a route that kept them out of sight of Lorimor's office window. They wound their way through a cluster of drab, two-story military buildings.

Just beyond the buildings they reached an enormous, wide-open space. A network of asphalt runways snaked before them, for what seemed like miles. It looked as though some of them were in steady use, but others were as neglected as Lorimor had described them. The heat-buckled asphalt was losing its battle against cracks and weeds, and many of the lights that lined either side had fallen.

In the distance, almost to the horizon, Frank spotted a group of large, squat buildings. They were dark and round-roofed, like a row of huge oil drums that had fallen on their sides and sunk halfway into the ground.

"There are our hangars," Frank said.

Joe counted them silently. "Ten of them—this is going to take forever."

"And for all we know, there may be even more behind those."

A loud, commanding voice made them turn. "May I help you?"

"Oh, no, sir," Joe said, facing a towering, grim-faced air force sergeant. "We're civil engineering assistants doing a survey on the wear-and-tear of the NZE-809 runways."

The sergeant smiled. "Well, it's about time they sent someone to take care of this mess. You go right ahead."

"Thank you, sir," Joe replied.

"Thank *you,*" Frank said to Joe under his breath as they began walking toward the hangars.

When they got there, they started on the far right. The wide, aircraft-size doors for each hangar were shut tight, but on the first hangar Frank found a small side door that was open.

That hangar was completely empty, a yawning, musty cavern of wood and steel. The second was an indoor parking lot for what seemed like World War II–vintage trucks and jeeps, all covered with a thick layer of dust. The third one was empty except for some battered office equipment stashed in a corner. The fourth echoed with the noise of bats.

With each hangar, they picked up their pace. At the sixth one, Joe said, "This is giving me the creeps. No one's been out here for years, Frank."

"I know. That's what makes it a perfect"—Frank reached for the door handle and pulled, but it wouldn't budge—"hiding place."

Above the knob was a shiny brass lock, covered with a sturdy, flat security plate. "A brand-new, state-of-the-art, deadbolt lock," Frank said. "You think there just might be something inside?"

He checked down the side of the building and saw a small window. "Let's try that," he said.

Joe got there first. He gave it a good, hard push and it opened.

They scrambled inside, dropping to the floor of the hangar. The shafts of light through the dust-encrusted windows illuminated two long sets of tire tracks. At the ends of the tracks were two large, white semitrucks—completely unmarked, without a trace of a company logo.

They raced to the semi that was nearest to them. Frank gripped the handle of the cargo door and yanked it open.

They peered inside. Large, rugged moving blankets were piled up just inside the door, along with thick ropes and a couple of dollies and hand trucks. At the far end of the trailer, padded with blankets and strapped to the wall near the cab of the truck, were a half dozen large containers.

And uncovered at the bottom of one container were the words Caution: Radioactive Substance.

"Bingo!" Joe shouted. "Look what we found!"

A loud crack echoed through the hangar—the sound of a heavy deadbolt being unlocked. Frank and Joe instinctively crouched down.

As the hangar door slowly swung open, it sent in another shaft of light—and the long shadow of a man.

The click, click, click of the man's shoes resounded as he walked closer. "Stand up, boys," came a familiar voice.

Slowly Frank and Joe stood.

"Look what I found!" said the man.

Inside his office, Captain Lorimor had sounded gruff and unpleasant. But now, booming into the rafters of the empty hangar, his voice was downright diabolical. As he moved closer, his stony face was distorted by a wide and wild grin.

"Imagine happening to see a couple of spies all the way out here," he purred. "Too bad they tried to escape, otherwise I wouldn't have had to shoot them."

Slowly, deliberately, with a steady hand, Lorimor pointed a revolver at Frank's heart.

Chapter

Eighteen

Y<small>OU WOULDN'T DO THAT,</small>" Frank said, staring into Lorimor's eyes.

"You don't need to dare me, boy," Lorimor replied.

"Others know about our investigation, Captain," Frank said. "If you kill us, they'll suspect you for everything you've done. You've already got one death on your hands. Don't push your luck."

"Oh?" Lorimor looked amused. "I wasn't aware of killing anyone else. Pray tell what your highly professional investigation came up with."

"The evidence leads right to Dr. Langford,"

Joe cut in. "He suspected the nuclear stuff, so you and your buddy Fripp took care of him Saturday night."

Lorimor swung his gun to Joe. "Two points for finding out that my partner is Fripp," he said. "But your detective methods are slipshod. I don't even know who this Dr. Langford is—excuse me, *was*. And if he did know about our little stash of goodies, then his murderer saved me a lot of trouble. Besides, Fripp and I were both at a function in Altus that night. There are, oh, thirty witnesses who would testify to that. Not to mention my wife and son, who went home with me, where we all enjoyed a full and pleasant night's sleep."

Frank was sweating. He knew Lorimor was telling the truth. There was no reason for him to lie to two condemned people. Langford must have been killed for some other reason, by someone else.

But right then there was a more important murder case to worry about. One that was about to happen. His and Joe's.

"Whatever you're up to, Lorimor, it's not going to work," Frank said. "A lot of people know who we are and where we are—like the Network."

Lorimor let out a deep, bellowing laugh. "The Network! That's a good one. That really scares me." He leaned in close to Frank.

"When my project is over, two-bit organizations like the Network won't survive. This country needs men who can act, who can prepare, who can defend—not pointy-headed intelligence bureaucrats who hire children to do their dirty work."

Frank thought fast. Lorimor was a fanatic, obsessed with a need to win at all costs. As long as they challenged him, made him work to win, he wouldn't shoot. "I thought you were a patriot, Lorimor," he said, suddenly smiling. "But now I know what you are. An enemy of democracy. I see what your so-called 'project' is—hoarding nuclear materials for your own terrorist schemes!"

Joe stared at him as if he were insane.

Lorimor pushed his gun against Frank's nose. "Watch what you say about terrorism. *I'm* the one who stuck his neck out for American hostages when everyone else ran away."

Lorimor remained still for a moment, his eyes staring coldly, his finger gripping the trigger. Frank fought to keep himself from shaking.

Then, slowly, Lorimor lowered the gun. "I'm going to tell you something about patriotism and democracy. I'd hate for you to go without knowing the cause you died for." He dropped his hands to his sides, still holding the gun.

Frank saw his brother swallow deeply. Out of the corner of his eye, he looked into the back of the trailer, taking a quick inventory of what was inside.

"Democracy, my friends, is like a porcupine in a forest of lions. It's a gentle, peace-loving creature, but because of its quills, the lions leave it alone. But if it lost its quills, or if they became soft instead of sharp, why, the porcupine would be nothing more than a cuddly little ball of meat. And *wham*—the lions have the dinner they've been eyeing all along!"

"What does a porcupine have to do with your stealing nuclear material?" Joe demanded.

Lorimor spun around and practically stuck his face in Joe's. "It's a metaphor! Must I spell it out? The porcupine represents the United States. Its quills are the military. Get it?"

He backed away and began pacing. "Look at these empty hangars—a waste of taxpayers' money! Where are the fighter jets that are supposed to be in here? Where is the NZE-809? I'll tell you where—sitting half-finished in assembly plants like rotting dinosaur skeletons. Why? Because some slick urban politician has convinced the public that we don't *need* to be protected!" His nostrils flared with rage, and then he seemed to get himself under control. "They don't know how vulnerable this country is to terrorism." His lips curled into a smile, and Frank immediately felt a cold chill. "I am about to teach them."

Lorimor went to the semi and gestured to the containers inside. "You know how much I can get for these on the black market? More money than you boys will ever see in your lives!"

Joe's eyes widened. "You're going to sell that stuff? To an enemy? That's treason!"

"You're angry about the military's weakness," Frank said, "so you sabotage your own country."

Lorimor chuckled. "No wonder you're civilians—no concept of strategic thinking. I'm saving the country from its own stupidity. If people can see how easy it is for a terrorist group to get its hands on nuclear materials, then they'll understand how important a strong military is! Then they'll force the politicians to vote for increased spending!"

"What's the difference?" Joe said. "The terrorists will already have the stuff!"

"All the more reason to start spending fast," Lorimor replied. "With only a few billion, we can blow them off the map before they figure out how to open the containers!"

"And in the meantime, you walk away with the money," Joe said.

"What should I do?" Lorimor said with a

sardonic laugh. "Give it back to the terrorists? Nothing wrong with making a little profit off the enemy, is there?"

Lorimor's eyes were like beacons. His skin was flushed with excitement. Frank knew there was no reasoning with him. "I see," Frank said, scrunching up his brow. "I have to admit, it is a pretty brilliant idea, if you can pull it off."

Joe shot him a look, but didn't say anything. Frank knew his brother had caught on.

"Yes, it is," Lorimor said. He beamed with a self-satisfied smile. "Although I must say, it was Greg Fripp who planted the seed. He told me about a cache of nuclear waste on the old Indian's land. I immediately saw the potential —but while I was figuring out my plan, Whiteshirt began complaining about spirits, or some such nonsense. Told everyone in the press how that patch of land couldn't be farmed, how the vegetation turned funny colors. We thought he might trigger an investigation, so we dug up the waste and moved it to a place way up on Quartz Mountain. We were about ready to put it up for bids on the black market when, lo and behold, these two truck shipments came through! It was too good to pass up."

Frank nodded. "Sort of like an omen."

"Exactly." Lorimor hiked himself up onto

the trailer floor. He sat there, facing the Hardys, with his legs dangling over the rear bumper and his back resting against the pile of blankets. "You know, you're brighter than I thought—and so young. Too bad the Network got ahold of you."

Frank sighed. He took a couple of steps toward the truck, trying to look as if he were deep in thought. "I don't know," he said. "Maybe you have a point. Could you use someone like my brother and me? I mean, we do feel very strongly about our country—" He sensed Joe edging closer to the truck, right behind him. "And I've always thought that radical change requires radical thinking." He stared pleadingly at Lorimor's face. "You think we could talk?"

Lorimor shifted his gaze uncertainly from Frank to Joe. "How do I know you're not bluffing?"

"Captain Lorimor," Frank said, meeting him squarely in the eye, "Patrick Henry once said something like 'I only regret that I have but one life to lose for my country.' The way I see it, my brother and I can sacrifice our lives here, or we can give them over to the cause of democracy."

"You can use guys like us," Joe said. "Take us to your office and we'll sign a statement."

Lorimor pressed the heels of his hands

against the trailer floor to push himself back to the ground. "I'm not sure I—"

That was all Frank needed. He dove at Lorimor, hurling his shoulders into the man's chest.

A helpless "Oof!" was Lorimor's only response. Joe instantly lunged forward and grabbed the gun out of his hand. Throwing it to the floor, he wrapped his muscular arms around Lorimor's flailing legs.

Frank tried to immobilize Lorimor's upper body with a wrestling hold, but the older man overpowered him. With a snarl of rage, Lorimor grabbed Frank by the neck.

Frank sputtered helplessly. Lorimor's hands felt like metal claws.

"Frank!" Joe shouted. He threw himself on top of Lorimor, trying to pry his hands loose.

In the melee, Frank reached into the pile of blankets. Closing his fingers around the edge of one, he pulled.

The blanket tumbled onto Lorimor's face. "Mmph!" came the muffled response. His hands loosened their grip on Frank's throat.

Frank freed himself. When Lorimor threw off the blanket, Frank and Joe were waiting. They pummeled him with a barrage of well-placed punches, knocking him unconscious.

Quickly Frank and Joe grabbed the ropes from the floor of the truck and tied him up.

"Let's get out of here!" Frank said. He and

Joe ran to the door that Lorimor had left open. Outside, the captain's Jeep was waiting.

"This one *I'll* drive!" Joe said as he hopped into the driver's seat.

They sped down one of the runways. Winding their way back through the complex of buildings, they drove into the parking lot near Lorimor's office and pulled up next to their rented sedan.

Wasting no time, they switched cars. The squeal of tires mixed with the crunch of gravel as Frank and Joe drove away from Jackson Air Force Base, tense but alive.

On the highway, about five miles from the base, Frank began to relax. "I can't believe we pulled that off."

Joe was staring out the window, his face taut with concentration. "It was Nathan Hale," he finally said.

"Huh?"

"It was Nathan Hale who said, 'I only regret that I have but one life to lose for my country' —not Patrick Henry."

"Oh." Frank smiled for the first time since the early morning. "Good thing Lorimor didn't catch that one."

Joe stared back out the window. "I give him fifteen, maybe twenty minutes before he wakes up and breaks loose. What's our plan? Call the police?"

"We'll face too many questions. They'll believe Lorimor. We'd better deal with the Network directly."

Minutes later they drove into the resort parking lot and ran to their room. Frank pushed the door open and stepped on a folded sheet of yellow legal paper. He picked it up and read it with Joe.

AM IN MY ROOM—208.
COME RIGHT AWAY!

First things first. Frank grabbed the phone and called the Network, going through the ritual of code names once again.

"Hello?" came an unfamiliar voice.

"Lifeline?" Frank asked.

"Who? Oh, wait. Lifeline—that's L, I, F, E . . ." Frank rolled his eyes as he heard individual loud clicks on a keyboard. "Mr. Hardy is the one who uses that nickname."

"Yes, I am Frank Hardy!" Frank said, trying to contain his anger. "Will you please put him on the line?"

"He's away from his desk, sir. May I take a message?"

"Yes! Tell him to have Captain Lorimor at Jackson Air Force Base arrested right away, whatever it takes—along with Greg Fripp, a lawyer in Altus."

"Spell it, please."

"A, L, T, U, S!" Frank was practically shouting.

"No, Fripp."

"F, R, I, P, P!"

"Will he know what this is in reference to?"

"Yes! Yes! Just tell him it's urgent—and tell him to call as soon as he gets in!" He slammed down the phone. "Our immediate future is not looking too secure, Joe."

"Maybe Lorimor was right about the Network," Joe remarked.

"Let's go see Nancy," Frank said, "before Lorimor shows up here with a fleet of attack planes."

They ran to the other wing of the hotel and found Nancy sitting on her bed, talking with George and Sky. Beside her lay the Geiger counter.

In a feverish flurry of words they exchanged their stories. But as Frank described what Lorimor had said in the hangar, Sky's face grew steadily paler. Frank couldn't help notice.

"Are you all right, Sky?" he asked.

"I didn't imagine Greg Fripp would be involved," she said. "My grandfather went to see him this morning. When I asked him why, all he would say was that it was urgent business." She looked at Frank desperately. "I wonder if my grandfather does know something about the nuclear waste."

"When did he leave?" Frank asked.

"Hours ago," Sky said. "He should be back by now. This is usually his time to rest."

"We've got to see him," Frank said. "If Fripp thinks your grandfather will stand in the way of his crazy plan, then your grandfather's life is in great danger!"

Chapter

Nineteen

H E'S HERE!" Sky said when she saw White-shirt's battered old pickup in front of her house.

Frank pulled up quickly, jouncing right over the dirt yard and up to the front door. The four of them rushed out of the car and into the house.

"Grandfather?" Sky called out, running into his bedroom.

Immediately she came back out. "He's gone, but I can tell he's been here—his reading glasses are in his room, and I know he took them this morning."

"Where could he be, Sky?" Nancy asked. "A store, a club, a friend's house?"

"I—I don't know," Sky said. "He never misses a nap. Maybe Mrs. Redriver saw him."

She ran outside and hurried to the next house over. The others followed. An old, craggy-faced woman answered, the same woman who had eyed Nancy and Joe suspiciously two days before when they had investigated Sky and Whiteshirt's house.

"Hi, Mrs. Redriver," Sky said breathlessly. "Did you see my grandfather today?"

The old woman stared past Sky to take in Nancy and the others one by one. Finally she said, "Yep. He got back here, oh, maybe an hour ago. Didn't come by, though. Seemed pretty tired—least I thought so."

"And then what?" Sky pressed. "Did he leave again?"

Mrs. Redriver nodded. "Them two men came—in some brand-new pickup, dark blue, nice one. Only about, oh maybe five minutes ago. He left with them."

"What two men?" Sky asked, her voice rising.

"You know, the fella you two been spending a lot of time with—the little bald guy with the suit who was in the newspaper picture with you. Looks like a half-blood."

"You mean Greg Fripp!" Sky said. "And the other man?"

The old woman shrugged. "Never seen him before. Short, short hair, looked like an army man."

Frank and Joe eyed each other. "Lorimor!" Joe blurted.

Sky put her hand to her mouth, backing away from the door. Her eyes were wide with fright. "What are they going to do to him?"

"Did you see which way they went, Mrs. Redriver?" Nancy asked urgently.

"There," the woman said, pointing down the road toward the dig. "They were going pretty fast, too."

Before the woman could finish speaking, Frank was running to the car. "Let's hightail it!" he shouted.

In seconds they were speeding away from the house, leaving Mrs. Redriver to shake her head with confusion.

Frank's speedometer edged into the danger zone as they shot down the highway. When he pulled off the road to drive to the dig, the car sent up a huge cloud of dust.

As they approached, several of the volunteers glanced up curiously.

"Anybody see a brand-new, dark blue pickup stop by here a few minutes ago?" Nancy called out.

There were a few shaking heads, a few blank stares. "It didn't stop" came a voice to the left.

They spun around to see Saul, leaning

against his shovel. He pointed toward the mountains. "They kept going. I think they went left at the fork—the road that leads up the mountain." His intelligent, freckled face was full of curiosity, but he didn't ask what the frantic teenagers were up to.

"They're taking him to the cave!" Sky exclaimed with horror.

"We're going to need help," Nancy said to Frank and Joe. "Saul, is Lieutenant Deerhunter around?"

"He was," Saul replied, "but he went off to get something to eat. He should be back any minute."

"Thanks." Nancy turned to George. "Can you wait for Deerhunter and bring him up to the cave as soon as he gets here?"

"You bet," George said.

"Great. Let's go, guys!"

Nancy, Sky, Frank, and Joe all got back into the car and took off.

Frank took a left at the fork. The road wound through the desert, then sloped upward toward the mountain. Before long, the asphalt ended and the car was bouncing along the dirt. "There it is!" Joe shouted.

Hidden behind a bush at the base of the mountain was a dark blue pickup.

Frank noticed the long scratch marks on the vehicle's right side. "I've seen this pickup before," he growled as they all got out of the car, "just outside my window on the way to a bridge abutment."

"Fripp must have seen us leave his office and followed us," Joe speculated.

"Well, now we can return the favor." Frank was the first in line behind Sky as she sprinted up the narrow dirt path. It wound upward over rocks and around clumps of thick brush and dry nettles.

As they climbed higher, Nancy started breathing heavily again. Behind her, the labored panting sounded like an overworked locomotive.

As if she were climbing stairs, Sky raced easily up until they lost sight of her.

"Do you know where to go, Nancy?" Joe called out.

"Yes," she replied, stretching the truth.

She followed a path that she hoped Sky had taken. Her lungs felt as if they would rip apart. When she inhaled, it was more of a gulp than a breath.

"We're—going to be—in great shape—to fight them!" Joe gasped.

When they got a few yards higher, Nancy spotted Sky crouching behind an outcropping of rock. The edge of the cliff was in sight above them.

Sky put a finger against her mouth, cautioning them to be quiet. They all crouched around her and listened.

From over the cliff, where the cave was, Nancy heard a frantic *chink, chink* noise.

On all fours, Sky slowly crept up the steep embankment.

Chink—chink— "Can't you go any faster?" came a gravelly voice.

"That's Lorimor," Frank whispered.

Then they heard Fripp's voice. "I—I don't know if this is really a good idea."

"Keep your emotions out of this!" thundered Lorimor. "Just dig! The old man wouldn't have had much time left on this earth anyway."

"Aiiiiiiieeee!" Sky shouted, wild with fury. She leaped over the cliff and disappeared.

"Come on!" Nancy yelled. She scrambled up to the edge and looked over.

Sky had fallen on top of her grandfather, who lay on the ground, tied up with rope. Frantically she tried to loosen the bonds. Behind her stood Lorimor, his face slack with shock. With lightning reflexes, he raised his shovel over his head.

"Sky, behind you!" Nancy shouted, jumping onto the platform.

Nancy grabbed the shovel handle as it swung down, but she was too late. With a sickening thud, it glanced against the back of Sky's head. She fell to the ground in a heap.

"Mmmmph . . . rrrgh!" Whiteshirt writhed on the ground, his anguished eyes riveted on his granddaughter.

Frank and Joe dropped to the platform behind Nancy. Lorimor squared around, facing them all. "You almost got me," he snarled at Frank. He dropped the shovel and instantly whipped out his revolver from its holster. "This time I'm leaving no room for error."

"Captain Lorimor, really!" Fripp said, looking pale.

"How deep are those holes, Fripp?" Lorimor asked. "Enough for four bodies?"

Nancy's eyes darted to the back of the cave. There, the tops of two large containers protruded from the ground.

"Where are you going to hide those now?" Joe asked.

Lorimor pointed the gun at him. "You ask too many questions—and I've revealed way too much to you already. Besides, think of how the ecology will improve once we remove these things. Your bones will be much more nutritious for the surrounding soil than these containers were."

"This is, ahem, going a bit far," Fripp said. "First of all, we can't fit all of them in there."

Lorimor glared at his partner. "How can you have cold feet now? This was your idea!"

"My idea?" Fripp snapped. "I saw the financial opportunity in these containers, and you assured me it wouldn't be a security risk. It was going to be profit from a forgotten commodity—clean, easy. Now you've gotten us into grand larceny, obstruction of interstate transportation, kidnapping, and five counts of murder! I'm a *lawyer,* Lorimor! You were supposed to leave details like this to *me!*"

Lorimor's face was becoming beet red. The veins in his neck were like steel rods. "You think I really need you?" he snarled. He whirled around, pointing the gun at Fripp's face.

Instantly Frank lunged. He tackled Lorimor around the legs, throwing him to the ground.

"You little—" Lorimor growled. He threw Frank off and whipped the gun around, taking aim.

But Joe was right behind his brother. *"No!"* he shouted. He grabbed Lorimor's right wrist, knocking his arm backward.

A shot rang out. The bullet disappeared harmlessly upward. Using both arms, Joe twisted Lorimor's wrist. Slowly Lorimor's fingers opened and the gun fell out onto the ground. Joe picked it up and tossed it over the cliff. It bounced down the steep embankment, clattering against the protruding rocks.

Now Lorimor had both hands free. Pushing Frank and Joe aside with a superhuman shove, he stood up. "You want hand-to-hand combat?" he said. "Well, you picked the wrong guy, suckers."

As the three of them circled one another, Nancy faced Greg Fripp. He lurched at her with his shovel, a wild look in his eye.

"Think about this," Nancy said, backing away. "At the very least, they'll disbar you. You'll spend years in prison. Your career will be ruined."

Fripp kept advancing. Nancy sensed that she was getting closer to the edge of the cliff.

"No," he said. "Some crimes are never solved. Many suspicious deaths are labeled suicide."

With that last word, he gripped the shovel handle with both hands and thrust it at Nancy crosswise.

She grabbed it and pushed back. But Fripp was strong, and he had momentum. Nancy couldn't help stepping backward. She was inches from the edge. If she could just plant her feet . . .

"Nancy!" Frank shouted, turning away from Lorimor.

Nancy felt her body drop. The ground beneath her was crumbling. She tried to shift her weight forward.

"Rrrraaaghhh!" Fripp shouted as he gave one last shove.

Suddenly the edge of the cliff gave way. A scream tore from Nancy's lungs as she plunged over the edge!

Chapter
Twenty

Nancy's body dropped like a lead weight. The last thing she saw was a look of utter horror in Greg Fripp's eyes.

Her hands flew over her head as she bounced against the side of the cliff and began to slide.

Then, suddenly, she hit something. She felt a sharp, numbing pain in her chest, and her arms instinctively reached out.

They closed around a thick, protruding root. Nancy clutched at it with all her strength. Her feet dangled below her.

Without thinking, she looked down. At the bottom of the long dropoff, a pile of boulders awaited her. In the center of it was the shiny glint of Lorimor's gun.

Nancy immediately looked up again. She swung her legs toward the cliff wall. Feeling with her toes, she found a tiny foothold. She anchored her feet as best she could. Closing her eyes, she swallowed hard, willing herself not to think about what would happen if she fell.

But her hands were starting to slip on the tapered, dirt-encrusted root. "Frank! Joe!" she called out.

On the ledge the Hardys were fighting with new strength. They had both seen Nancy fall. Lorimor stood his ground, protecting himself with his fists. But he was no match against the martial-arts skills of two people less than half his age. Frank and Joe's kicks snapped toward him from both sides in a coordinated attack.

Lorimor staggered backward, and Joe finished him with a well-placed, old-fashioned roundhouse punch.

Groaning, the captain crumpled to the ground.

Frank and Joe immediately ran to the edge of the cliff. Nancy was staring up at them, her hands slipping perilously toward the tip of the root. "Help!" she cried.

"Anchor me!" Joe said to his brother. As Joe lay flat on his stomach, leaning over the edge,

Frank scrambled behind him and grabbed his ankles. Sitting with his back angled slightly backward, he dug his own heels into the ground for support.

Joe reached down, the tips of his fingers a foot away from Nancy's.

With a sudden jerk, Nancy slipped a couple of inches down the root. "I can't hold on much longer!" she whispered.

"I need more slack!" Joe shouted.

Frank slid forward. Joe pushed himself farther over the edge so that his entire upper body was hanging down. He thrust his hand toward Nancy's.

His fingers closed firmly around her wrist. He felt his biceps strain as he pulled upward. Nancy reached with her other arm. She managed to link her fingers with his.

Now gripping with two hands, Joe yelled at the top of his lungs, "Pull!"

Frank yanked as hard as he could, using his back and legs for support. He inched backward, digging in his heels again and again. Slowly Joe and Nancy emerged over the crumbled edge of the cliff.

When Nancy's shoulders were over the top, she hoisted herself up. The three of them could do no more than pant breathlessly, their chests heaving up and down.

After a moment Nancy looked at Joe and

Frank. "Once again," she said shakily, "you two saved my life. Thanks."

Both brothers turned red. "Hey, you've saved our necks a few times, too," Joe mumbled. "Forget it."

Standing up, Nancy scanned the ledge. Sky and Lorimor were both motionless on the ground. Beside them, Whiteshirt lay in a semiconscious stupor.

Nancy ran over to Whiteshirt and untied his ropes and gag. "Thank you," he said, his voice barely audible. "See to . . . Sky."

"You just rest," she told the old man, rushing over to her friend. With Frank and Joe's help, she revived Sky.

Glassy-eyed, Sky looked around. When she saw her grandfather, she wrapped her arms around him.

As Sky broke into sobs, Nancy heard a rustling above them.

"Nancy?" came George's anxious call.

"We're here!" Nancy answered.

George's face peeked over the ridge. She looked around and said, "Uh-oh, looks like we missed all the action."

"Is Deerhunter with you?" Nancy asked.

"In a way—I think," George answered with a shrug. "Climbing hills isn't his specialty."

"Come on down," Nancy urged.

As George did so, she said, "I see only one

bad guy here. Lorimor, right? What happened to Fripp?"

"I was hoping you saw him," Nancy replied. "He must have escaped."

"Must have?" George asked. "You mean, you don't know where he is?"

Joe spoke up. "Frank and I were busy conquering Goliath over here, and Nancy was dangling from a root."

"What?" George's eyes widened.

"It's a long story," Frank said. "But if Lorimor wakes up before we get to the end of it, we're in big trouble." He knelt down and picked up the rope that had been used to tie up Whiteshirt. "Let's wrap him up for the police."

As he, Joe, and George began tying up Lorimor, Nancy went over to Sky. At that moment, they heard a crackling static noise from above the ledge.

It was answered by a breathless "Yeah— Deerhunter—here."

"Guess who finally got here," George remarked.

"Over the ledge, lieutenant!" Nancy called out.

Deerhunter appeared above them, holding a two-way radio to his ear. His face was drenched with sweat, his mouth practically hanging open as he wheezed from exhaustion.

He gave them a slight tip of the head, as if a full nod would be too much effort. "Got to—get back in—shape," he admitted.

"I recommend aerobic dancing," Joe quipped. Deerhunter just looked at him. "Can't you take a joke?" Joe muttered.

"One of them got away!" George said to Deerhunter. "The lawyer I told you about—Fripp!"

Deerhunter put his mouth to the radio. "I need backups now!"

As Joe and Frank gave Deerhunter a physical description of Fripp, Nancy turned to Sky. "Are you all right?"

"A headache you wouldn't believe," Sky answered, rolling her eyes. "But my grandfather seems okay." She smiled. "Thank you, Nancy."

Nancy looked over at Whiteshirt. How much of this had he known about? It occurred to her that a man as closely attuned to the land as Whiteshirt could hardly have missed the fresh digging marks from the waste containers that had been buried in the cave.

As if reading her thoughts, Whiteshirt looked at her. "Yes, I knew the cans were here," he said in his soft old-man's voice. "I found them a few days ago. They are the source of disharmony. They ruin the land and disturb the dead."

"If you knew they were here, why didn't you tell the authorities?" Nancy asked, frowning.

Whiteshirt shrugged. "The authorities must have brought them to my land in the first place," he said quietly. "Would they heed the wishes of an old Comanche now? No, the only thing I could do was try to turn the evil around myself, in the Comanche way."

Nancy nodded, feeling she understood him a little better. Whiteshirt might have some odd notions, but clearly he was not in the least bit crazy.

There was another question she wanted to ask him. "What made you go to Fripp today?"

"Who else besides my granddaughter knew about the cave? I showed Gregory Fripp this place myself," Whiteshirt responded. His eyes held a trace of bitterness. "I knew he must have put the cans here. I went to tell him he must undo the evil he had wrought."

Whiteshirt put a hand on Nancy's arm. "Now you are helping to turn the evil around," he said. "I can feel it leaving my land."

Out of the corner of her eye, Nancy could see the old nuclear waste containers. She would make sure they were taken away by the proper authorities. "Yes," she said, looking at Whiteshirt. "I can feel it, too."

For the first time, she noticed the necklace Whiteshirt was wearing—full of gold medallions. She wondered if Joe had seen it yet, and began thinking once again about Tod Langford's murder. This case, she knew, was far from over.

Forty-five minutes later, in front of the head-quarters tent, Nancy watched a police car pull away with Lorimor in the backseat. She breathed a sigh of relief.

Deerhunter, who had summoned the car by two-way radio, shook his head and muttered, "It was bad enough that he tried to sabotage his own government, but did he have to get caught in a place where he'd have to be *carried* down from?"

"Right," Nancy agreed, grinning at him.

"At least Fripp had the decency to run down so my men could pick him up on the highway," Deerhunter said.

He exhaled wearily and peered over his glasses at Nancy. "Get the lovebird in here, would you? We have things to talk about."

As he disappeared inside the tent, Nancy scanned a secluded spot near the top of the hill. There, Jim and Sky were sitting in the shade of a big boulder, her head nestled in his shoulder. He nodded attentively, occasionally kissing her forehead as she told him about what had happened.

Nancy hated to interrupt, but she'd rather it be her than Deerhunter. "Sky?" she said gently as she approached them. "It's time for our meeting."

"Oh, sure," Sky said. Turning to Jim, she said. "'Bye. I'll be back in a few minutes."

"Okay," Jim replied, unhooking his arm.

Sky stood up and accompanied Nancy to the tent. Inside, Deerhunter, Frank, Joe, and George were waiting. Deerhunter had his two-way radio pressed to his ear. "Right— It's all there?— Good. Yes, over." He pulled the radio away and hooked it to his belt. "My men found the two semis. The air force people are falling all over themselves. Nobody can believe Lorimor did it."

"Somehow I don't think he's going to be able to charm his way out of this one with the press," Frank said.

Deerhunter glanced at Nancy and Sky, who were standing by the tent flap. "Okay," he said, "let's start talking. This is what I've managed to store in my small policeman's brain: Fripp and Lorimor had a deal to sell the nuclear waste and the two truck shipments to a black-market bidder. Fripp figured he'd make some big money and Lorimor wanted to scare the country into believing we need bombs on every street corner. John Whiteshirt was giving them trouble, so they decided to off him. My question is, why did they kill Langford?"

"Well, Dr. Langford had this Geiger counter," Nancy began.

Frank cut her off. "They didn't know about it. They were never around the site to see it."

"Maybe they had a spy," George suggested.

Joe shook his head. "Lorimor was completely surprised when we mentioned it. He was all set to shoot us, and he was gloating about all the other stuff he did, so he didn't have any reason to lie."

"What about Whiteshirt?" Frank asked. "Joe, when you drove him back to his house, did you ask him about that necklace he was wearing?"

"You bet," Joe said. "It *was* the one that had been missing from the house. It has all its medallions. He said he had found it years ago in the cave, as if someone had left it there for him. He wears it whenever he has to do some sort of ritual."

Nancy sighed. "Well, there's really only one other person we haven't followed up on."

"Uh-oh," Joe said under his breath. He and Frank looked at Sky.

"Who?" she said, bewildered.

"Jim Haber," Nancy said levelly.

"What?" The cry came from Sky and George at the same time. "Jim would never kill anyone!" George protested.

"You're way off base," Sky said. "Jim worshipped Dr. Langford. He was crushed when he died."

"Well," Deerhunter cut in. "Let's see if he's a better actor or archaeologist." He pulled open the tent flap, scanned the dig site for Jim, then shouted, "Hey, Romeo! Come on over here for a second."

Nancy saw Sky cringe. "He's not too delicate, is he," Nancy whispered.

When Jim came into the tent, Deerhunter immediately fired a question at him. "Okay, Haber, I want to know where you were Saturday night."

The smile on Jim's face faded. "Working in my room until eleven or so, then sleeping."

"Until?" Deerhunter asked.

"Until someone woke me up to tell me about Dr. Langford, around six o'clock." He cocked his head at Deerhunter. "Now, wait a minute. You're not implying that—"

"Dr. Langford was murdered," Deerhunter told him, his face unreadable, "and you have a motive. I'm implying you have some explaining to do."

Jim turned his face away in disgust. "I can't believe this. Why me?"

Deerhunter shrugged. "Explain this," he said, seeming to change the subject. "Someone planted a rattlesnake in the luggage of a girl detective who was on his tail. Funny thing that you just happened to be there to retrieve it."

"*Retrieve* isn't the right word to describe

getting something you haven't put there in the first place," Jim said, his voice growing indignant. "And I *didn't* put it there in the first place! That's absurd!"

"Is it?" Deerhunter said. "What's in it for you, Haber? Now that Langford's out of the way, will you finally get credit for discovering the Red Clay People site—the credit that Langford stole from you?"

Jim was horrified. At a loss for words, he could only gape.

"Furthermore," Deerhunter went on, "why would you be dating a Comanche woman—an outspoken enemy of the dig? Maybe it was to deflect suspicion or to ensure that you could set up her grandfather for suspicion?"

"Lieutenant!" Sky blurted out. "You're way out of line! Have a heart!"

"Look," Jim said with a sigh of exasperation. "I know you have to suspect lots of people. But I swear to you I would be the last person in the world to do something like that." He glanced briefly at Sky. "I mean, what can I say? I have no witnesses, no hard proof. Just— my word."

"Just your word," Deerhunter repeated, sticking his hand in his pants pocket. Keys and coins jingled noisily as he searched around for something.

Finally Nancy had a chance to ask about

something that had been bothering her. "Jim," she said, "Saturday at dinner, when we started talking about the thefts and the cave-ins, we all noticed that you got kind of defensive, like you didn't want to talk about it. Was there a reason?"

Jim's eyebrows came together as he thought back. "Yes. You guys had started talking about Sky, mentioning how angry she had been with Langford. And I knew—" He bowed his head. "I knew that she had filled in those first two graves, even though I was sure she hadn't stolen anything. Well, I was furious at her. I even thought she might have sabotaged Vault One. I almost turned her in myself. But to think others might discover her involvement —that whole idea made me uncomfortable. I needed to talk to her myself."

"We had a big argument about it Monday night," Sky said. "There was so much we needed to iron out. He was livid with me. I was wrapped up in my militant beliefs, and so angry at myself for—" She looked down with an embarrassed smile. "For falling in love with someone involved in the desecration of the graves." She looked up at Jim and smiled. "But somehow we made up."

Nancy remembered seeing Jim and Sky arguing that night. They weren't lying about that. Jim's story was making sense.

"Let's get back on track here," Deerhunter said, extracting his hand from his pocket. He held out his palm to Jim. "Recognize this?"

In it was the shining gold medallion that had been in Langford's hand.

Jim took it and brought it into the light of the open tent flap. He examined it carefully, turning it end over end. "No. I don't recall ever seeing this before."

"Interesting," Deerhunter said. "Considering that it's a Red Clay People artifact, found in one of your trenches."

Jim looked confused. "I don't know who told you that," he said, scrutinizing the coin again. "This design is definitely Mayan—and from about two centuries after the Spiro and the Red Clay People disappeared."

"Are you sure?" Nancy asked.

"As sure as I know my name," Jim replied.

"How do you know?" Deerhunter demanded.

"I'm an archaeologist," Jim said calmly. "If I didn't know how to identify signature artifacts like this, I wouldn't be worth much, would I?"

"Answer me this, then," Deerhunter said. "Isn't Dr. Ottman one of the country's leading experts in Mayan artifacts?"

"If not *the* leading expert," Jim shot back.

"Then how do you explain that it was Dr.

Ottman who told me the coin was from the Red Clay People?"

The question came out as dry and muted as anything else that had been said in the hot, cramped tent. But to Nancy, it echoed like the clang of a bell.

"You must have misunderstood—" Jim began to say.

Nancy cut him off. "No," she said. "I know who committed the murder!"

Chapter

Twenty-One

DEERHUNTER LEVELED HIS GAZE at Nancy. "Do you?" he said.

"Yes. And," Nancy continued, "I think you'll agree with me, Lieutenant!"

"What are you talking about? Who is it, Nancy?" George asked excitedly.

Nancy took a moment to piece together her thoughts, which were snapping into place like a jigsaw puzzle. "It was Dr. Ottman."

Deerhunter frowned. "Just because he mis-identified a coin? Maybe he didn't look closely at it."

"It's not just that," Nancy said. "Think about his relationship with Dr. Langford. Remember what you told me, George? Jim had described that Mayan dig fifteen years ago, the one that Dr. Ottman had headed with Dr. Langford."

"Right," George said, her eyes lighting up. She looked at Jim. "You said that Dr. Langford had gotten the credit for that dig, even though Dr. Ottman had done all the work."

"Well, most of the work," Jim said, defending his former mentor.

"Anyway, it was a well-known story. Another digger—Saul—mentioned the same thing," Nancy resumed. "So there's probably some truth in it. Think of it. Dr. Ottman was older than Dr. Langford, and he was the one who brought Langford into the dig. It was to be the height of Dr. Ottman's career. They were on the verge of making their big find when Dr. Ottman got sick—food poisoning. While he was in the hospital, Dr. Langford finished off what Dr. Ottman had begun. All of a sudden, headlines! TV interviews! Big feature articles in magazines! 'Key to Mayan Past Found by Young Archaeologist!'"

Deerhunter had become quietly thoughtful. "Go on," he said slowly.

Nancy shrugged. "Before you knew it, Dr. Langford was a full professor. Dr. Ottman *still* hasn't become one. All these years he's worked in Dr. Langford's shadow. His resentment must have built and built. And now, on the verge of major publicity for the Red Clay People dig, Dr. Ottman must have been thinking, If only I could steal *his* thunder this time!"

"But did Ottman really hate Langford enough to kill him?" Frank asked.

Jim spoke up. "Dr. Ottman's basically close-mouthed and a little paranoid. He keeps that junk around his neck because he's afraid someone'll pickpocket him. Imagine—here! And you know the way he always looks angry at everything. How can you know what a person like that is really thinking? I do know that a full professorship is an obsession with him. He once did imply to me that he thought Tod had caused his food poisoning at the Mayan dig. But that's just like him—he says things like that."

"Well, let me bring him in right now," Deerhunter said. "We'll have it out."

"He's back at the resort," Jim said. "Preparing for another lecture tonight."

"What's his room number?" Deerhunter asked. "I'll talk to him there."

"No," Nancy said suddenly. "I have a better idea, if you'll allow it."

Deerhunter raised his eyebrows. "Let's hear it," he ordered.

Nancy turned to Jim. "May I have the coin?"

"Sure," Jim said, giving it to her.

"I think we should break for dinner and be the first ones in the lecture hall tonight," Nancy said.

"Wait a second—" Deerhunter protested.

"You and your officers, of course, will be the key people," Nancy continued. "Hear me out. If it's a dumb plan, we can change it."

As Nancy outlined her idea, Deerhunter nodded reluctant assent.

"Good evening. Today we're going to discuss further the notion of cross-cultural assimilation through architectural detail."

Dr. Ottman's voice was a monotonous drone, but this time Nancy wasn't sleepy. She sat attentively, expectantly.

To her right, Joe was walking down the aisle. He was dressed neatly in a polo shirt and chinos, which were blackened around the pockets. As he sat next to Frank in an empty seat, Nancy and George looked over at him.

"Everything okay?" Nancy asked.

Joe nodded confidently.

"Nice pants," George remarked.

Joe quickly turned his hands around and held them out to George. "That's what happens when your hands are dirty."

"Yuck," George said with a grimace. "What were you doing?"

Nancy shushed them. Her attention was riveted to the front of the room. She watched Jim load the slide projector, turn its lamp on, then walk to the light switch at the back of the room.

As he passed Nancy's row, he gave her a small, almost imperceptible wink and held up his palm.

"I saw that," whispered George.

"It was for all of us, not just you," Joe said.

George shot him a disdainful sneer. "Give it up, Joe. Just because you're heartbroken over Sky doesn't mean—"

Frank cleared his throat loudly. "Guys—"

"Can we keep it down, please!" Dr. Ottman's voice rang out.

"Shhh!" Nancy whispered, her face set. The lights went out, and Jim made his way to the seat next to the projector. He grabbed the remote control and flicked on the first slide.

As Dr. Ottman lectured, Nancy kept her eyes glued to the screen. She carefully kept count of the slides. Jim had held up his entire palm—all five fingers. That meant she had to watch for the fifth slide.

Three . . . "Here we see the Spiro water boy figure juxtaposed with that of the Maya," Dr. Ottman explained. Nancy tuned out the rest of the description, waiting impatiently.

Four . . . "We notice the slight devolution of

the art as the Spiro are conquered by the less-refined Red Clay People."

Five! For a moment Dr. Ottman just stared at the slide of a pottery design that Jim had secretly slipped in. "Hmm, I don't know what this is doing here. It's from a different collection."

Nancy nudged Joe, who called out, as they had planned, "Could you tell us what it is? It's kind of cool."

"Well," Ottman said, "it's a figure from a much later Mayan period, a rather mystical, complicated symbol we'll talk about some other time."

"Haven't you shown that design to us before?" Frank asked. "On a medallion or something?"

Dr. Ottman exhaled impatiently. He fingered his necklace of keys and other paraphernalia. "Yes, I sometimes wear one for—for good luck. That's probably what you saw. Now, if we can have the next slide—"

"Oh!" Nancy said, jumping up from her seat. "You mean this one?" She held the coin high in the air. "The one that was found in Dr. Langford's hand after he died?"

A stone-cold silence enveloped the room. Even in the semidarkness, Nancy could see the color drain from Dr. Ottman's face. His hand dropped from his necklace.

A low, confused murmuring started sweeping through the audience. Frank and Joe quietly began inching toward the aisle.

Suddenly Dr. Ottman bolted toward a fire exit just beyond the screen. Jim lunged for him but tackled the screen instead. As it collapsed to the floor, it blocked Frank and Joe's path. "Watch it!" Frank shouted, leaping over it.

Joe collided with him in the air. Frank landed on his side and bounced to his feet in a commando roll. When he sprang up he was at the door, watching Dr. Ottman's back recede into the darkness outside.

"Where's Deerhunter? Where's our backup?" Joe asked frantically. Frank shrugged, already on the move. There was no point now in wondering what had happened to the officer who should have been guarding the exit.

As Frank and Joe sprinted out the door, Nancy and George were right behind them. The night was cool, but Nancy hardly noticed. Dr. Ottman was yards ahead of them, running with surprising speed.

"Get him!" Nancy yelled.

When he rounded the corner of the resort, he was attacked. Sky had heard Nancy's shout and timed her tackle perfectly. Dr. Ottman landed hard on the pavement.

There was a flash of silver as something flew out of his jacket pocket. It hit the ground with a metallic clatter.

"It's a gun!" George shouted.

Nancy, George, Frank, and Joe dove for it at the same time.

But Dr. Ottman got there first. "Get back!" he barked, scrambling to his feet. He grabbed Sky by the arm and pulled her against his body. Gritting his teeth with savage fury, he pressed the gun to Sky's head. "Don't think I won't do it!" he cried. Looking quickly over his shoulder at the parking lot, he said, "Now, I'm going to my car. If any of you move, I'm shooting!"

He walked backward, dragging Sky along. Nancy stood frozen. Her eyes darted out to the road beyond the lot. It wound to the left, disappearing around another section of the resort. Then it emerged on the other side, leading directly onto the long, straight highway. If Dr. Ottman got there, it would be impossible to catch up.

"Someone call the cops!" one of the volunteers shouted.

"Don't try it!" Dr. Ottman shouted. "I want to see all of you standing where you are until we're out of sight!"

He shoved Sky in through the driver's side and pushed her over. Then he hopped in himself and slammed the door. Nancy could see him fumbling for his keys. She felt her stomach begin to flutter. Once again, her eyes darted out to the road and back. What had happened to Deerhunter?

Now Dr. Ottman was sticking his key in the ignition. There was a muffled sob from one of the volunteers in the crowd. Angry muttering started from the back.

Dr. Ottman turned the key.

The engine turned over once—then protested. The noise was halfway between a wheeze and a scrape.

Frantically, Dr. Ottman tried again. Nancy cast a sidelong glance at Joe. He was staring straight ahead. He wore a satisfied look.

Vrroooooom! Suddenly the roar of an engine filled the air.

"Oh, no," moaned someone in the crowd.

Then there were two engines. Then three. Lights flooded the surrounding area. Tires shrieked against the asphalt.

"Give it up, Ottman!" an amplified voice boomed.

From around the hidden side of the hotel, three police cars emerged. Dr. Ottman threw open his door and ran for the road. As one of the cars followed him, Lieutenant Deerhunter hopped out of another, brandishing a rifle.

Craackk!

The gunshot sounded like a sonic boom in the nighttime stillness. Dr. Ottman stopped in his tracks.

Deerhunter lowered his gun. "The next one won't be in the air, Ottman!" he shouted. Slowly Dr. Ottman turned around, his hands raised.

Nancy ran to the car and opened the passenger door. Frank, Joe, and George were right on her heels. "Are you all right?" Nancy asked.

Sky rubbed her head and smiled. "After today, I may have to change my hat size—but otherwise, I'm fine."

Nancy laughed, then turned to Joe. "Good work."

Joe reached into his pocket and pulled out three spark plugs. "Every once in a while I have a decent idea." He threw the plugs on Ottman's dashboard. "They were almost shot, anyway."

Nancy looked over her shoulder to see a police officer frisking Ottman while Deerhunter slapped handcuffs on him. For a moment she caught Deerhunter's eye. For the first time since she'd met him, he flashed an honest smile.

A few minutes later Deerhunter ambled over to Nancy, George, and the Hardys. "Sorry. A bureaucratic debate about this idea of yours held us up," he said matter-of-factly. "I figured you could handle it yourselves, though. You did okay, even if you messed up at the end."

Joe bristled. "Yeah, well, I thought we handled it pretty well, considering that we had no backup," he retorted.

Deerhunter gave Joe an expressionless look. "You've got to learn to take a joke, Hardy," he said. Then he winked and walked away.

Chapter

Twenty-Two

So it was Ottman all the way, huh?" George said as she loaded her duffel bag into Jim's pickup for the ride to the airport the next day.

"That's what Deerhunter says," Nancy replied, heaving her own duffel bag inside. "Dr. Ottman confessed everything. It seems that Dr. Langford wrote an article for release to all the major media, and in it he barely even mentioned Dr. Ottman as part of dig personnel. Dr. Ottman saw this as part of Dr. Langford's personal campaign to sabotage his career. He figured if he could get the press to come to the site, he'd be able to get some publicity for himself. So he stole all those artifacts so the press would take an interest. Also, he thought it would be bad press for Langford. The head of the dig couldn't manage his own expedition."

"Langford must have found out," Sky speculated.

"Exactly," Nancy said. "Dr. Ottman also knew that Dr. Langford was suspicious about radioactivity at the site, so he lured Dr. Langford out to Vault Thirteen Saturday night, saying he had seen some strange lizard mutations or something. He attacked Dr. Langford, and in the struggle Dr. Langford grabbed his necklace. Everything went flying, but Dr. Langford held on to the medallion."

"Thus throwing suspicion on me and my grandfather," Sky murmured.

"Dr. Ottman clubbed Dr. Langford over the head," Nancy went on. "That blow actually killed Dr. Langford, but Dr. Ottman didn't realize it. Quickly he scooped up what fell from his necklace, but he didn't notice the medallion was missing. Then he caved in the wall of the trench, thinking he'd suffocate Dr. Langford and make his death look like an accident. He knew about Sky's protests, so he planted that threatening note, hoping to incriminate her. Then, somehow he found out I was asking questions, and he planted that rattlesnake to scare me."

Jim grimaced. "Ugh, that was my fault, I

think. I mentioned our dinner conversation to him."

"Big help you were," Sky teased, nudging him in the arm.

Just then Frank and Joe's car pulled up beside them. They were taking a different flight, but they were going with the others to see Nancy and George off at the airport. "Ready to go?" Frank called out from the driver's seat.

Jim and Sky exchanged a look. "There are three things I wanted to tell you before we leave," Sky said, "since we'll probably be too rushed at the airport to talk."

"Shoot," Frank said. "But hurry."

"Well, number one," Sky began, "my grandfather got a call from the government today. Publicity about Fripp and Lorimor's plot is leaking out, and they promised him they'd do all they could to clean up any trace of radiation."

"Yeah!" Joe shouted, thrusting his fist out of the car window. "What's number two?"

Sky clutched Jim's arm. "Number two is that Mr. James Haber, now the acting head of the Red Clay People dig, has promised to rebury the bones of the dead and not dig up any more. And number three is an extension of number two."

"How could anything top number two?" Nancy said, smiling.

"Here's how," Sky said with a radiant grin. "I said yes to his proposal of marriage this morning!"

"Congratulations!" Nancy shouted. She threw her arms around both of them as Frank and Joe hooted loudly and hopped out of their car. When Nancy let go, George took her turn with hugs. If the news of the engagement bothered her at all, it didn't show.

As Nancy watched Frank and Joe happily pump the couple's hands, she beamed. When she first came to Oklahoma, she had jumped into an ugly clash of two cultures. Now she knew that the next time she came, it would be for a wedding. Two members of the two cultures were taking a step that would bring them closer to a mutual understanding.

It was about time.